The Case of the
Disappearing Diamonds

Larry had just pointed the plane back toward the airport when a cracking sound caused the small aircraft to shudder. The shudder turned into a violent and steady shake.

Nancy and Ned were jolted back and forth in their seats when a second crack sounded with tremendous force and black fluid spattered across the windshield.

"It's the oil pump!" Larry shouted. He clutched the wildly vibrating steering wheel tightly in both hands. "Hang on! We're going down!"

Nancy Drew Mystery Stories

Available from MINSTREL Books

NANCY DREW MYSTERY STORIES®

NANCY DREW®

THE CASE OF THE DISAPPEARING DIAMONDS

CAROLYN KEENE

A MINSTREL™ BOOK

PUBLISHED BY POCKET BOOKS

A MINSTREL PAPERBACK *ORIGINAL*

 A Minstrel Book published by
POCKET BOOKS, a division of Simon & Schuster, Inc.,
1230 Avenue of the Americas, New York, N.Y. 10020

ISBN: 0-671-64896-9

Produced by Mega-Books of New York, Inc.

First Minstrel Books printing November, 1987

10 9 8 7 6 5 4 3 2 1

Contents

THE CASE OF THE DISAPPEARING DIAMONDS

1

Meeting Monica Crown

Nancy Drew heard the front door close with a bang. Then a voice called out, "I'm home!"

Nancy hurried out of the dining room, where she had been setting the table for dinner. She saw her father, Carson Drew, place his briefcase on the hall table.

"Dinner's almost ready," Nancy told her father. Then she asked, "What was your Sunday meeting about?"

Mr. Drew shrugged out of his raincoat and hung it up in the hall closet. He gave his daughter a quick kiss and said, "Let's go into the den and I'll tell you all about it. Part of it concerned you."

"Me?" Nancy asked curiously, as she followed her father down the hall.

When they got to the den, Carson Drew sank into his favorite leather easy chair. Nancy perched herself on the arm of the leather sofa

1

opposite him and looked expectantly at her father.

Mr. Drew said, "Have you ever heard of Monica Crown?"

Nancy smiled and said, "Who *hasn't* heard of Monica Crown? I mean, she's probably the most famous mystery writer in America. She's lived in River Heights for years, but almost no one ever sees her." Nancy's blue eyes opened wide. "You met with Monica Crown today?"

Carson Drew nodded. "She insisted on a Sunday appointment. Mrs. Crown is a very private person, and she didn't want anyone else to be in the office when we met." He paused for a moment, then said, "She asked about you."

Nancy stared at her father. "Monica Crown asked about *me?*" she said in disbelief.

Her father nodded. "She told me she's followed all of your cases in the newspaper. She's very impressed. She feels that you're a fine detective and she needs your help."

"Monica Crown must be in some sort of trouble if she needs a detective," Nancy replied thoughtfully. Then she asked her father, "What did she want to see you about?"

"Mrs. Crown is planning to transfer all of her personal papers and legal documents from a law office in New York to my firm, here in River Heights. As of today, I'm Monica Crown's lawyer."

"That's terrific!" Nancy said, pleased for her

2

father. "She'll be a really important client."
Nancy frowned. "I wonder why she needs my
help."

"All she would tell me," Mr. Drew said, "is
that it has something to do with her daughter,
Karen."

"Oh, right," Nancy replied, nodding. "I remember reading that Karen Crown was arrested
for robbery a few months ago."

"Mrs. Crown didn't discuss the facts of the
case with me. All she would say is that she's
convinced Karen is innocent—"

"And she wants me to prove it," Nancy finished, her eyes sparkling with excitement.

Nancy's father nodded. "Correct. Mrs. Crown
also wanted to know if you could make an appointment to see her at her home tomorrow
afternoon." He handed his daughter a business
card with Monica Crown's address and phone
number on it.

Nancy looked at the card and said, "I'll make
the appointment right after dinner, Dad." She
grinned at her father. "This sounds like it could
be a really interesting case."

Mr. Drew laughed. "That's what you say about
all of your cases, Nancy." Carson Drew looked at
his daughter affectionately. He sometimes wondered if any other father and daughter could
possibly be as close as they were. Nancy's mother
had died fifteen years before, when Nancy was
three years old. Since then, Nancy had been

3

raised with love and affection by her father and the Drews' housekeeper, Hannah Gruen.

Just then, the door to the den opened. Hannah Gruen stood in the doorway. "Okay, you two, I hope your conference is over because dinner's ready," she said.

"Great!" Mr. Drew said. "I'm ready for your fabulous peach cobbler, Hannah."

"Turkey and trimmings first, peach cobbler *later*," Hannah reminded him as they walked into the dining room.

During dinner, Nancy and Mr. Drew filled Hannah in on their conversation in the den. "I hope you can solve Monica Crown's problem as quickly as possible," Hannah said to Nancy. "I hate to think of anything keeping her away from her writing."

"Do you read Monica Crown's books, too, Hannah?" Carson Drew asked in surprise.

"She's my favorite mystery writer," Hannah replied. She added with a smile, "I don't spend *all* my time cooking."

Nancy laughed. "I promise to solve the Monica Crown case as fast as I can, Hannah."

The next day, after lunch, Nancy raced upstairs to change for her appointment with Monica Crown. For her meeting with the famous author, Nancy decided to wear a camel-colored pleated wool skirt and a white sweater. She brushed her long reddish blond hair until it shone. After quickly checking her appearance in the mirror, she was ready to go. She left the house with a feeling of anticipation.

Monica Crown's estate was located in the rolling hills three miles outside downtown River Heights. However, Nancy had no time to admire the huge home. As soon as she had switched off the engine of her blue sports car, the massive front door of the mansion opened. A woman in a black dress stood in the doorway.

As Nancy walked up the front steps, the woman said, "Good afternoon. I'm Mrs. Crown's housekeeper. Mrs. Crown is waiting for you in the library."

Nancy couldn't help but smile. The library seemed like just the right place to meet a famous writer. When they reached the library, Nancy wanted to look around the wood-paneled room at the walls covered with thousands of books, but she was unable to take her eyes away from Monica Crown. The author's presence dominated the room.

Mrs. Crown rose from a high-backed antique chair and walked briskly across the room. With a nod she dismissed the housekeeper. Then she extended her right hand to Nancy and said in a low, clear voice, "Thank you for coming."

Nancy shook Monica Crown's hand, taking in every detail about the appearance of the older woman. Monica Crown was a tall, elegant woman who looked to be in her mid-fifties. She had short blond hair and a rosy complexion. She wore a white silk blouse, a black velvet blazer, and matching pants.

"Please sit down," the author said, indicating a comfortable sofa by a window. She smiled at her guest. "From what I've read about you, Nancy, you are an excellent detective."

"Well, I have managed to solve a few cases," Nancy said modestly. "But I want you to know I'm a big fan of yours, Mrs. Crown. I've read every book you've ever written."

"Thank you, my dear." Mrs. Crown's smile faded as she got down to the business at hand. "I know you're curious about why I need your help. Perhaps you recall reading about my daughter, Karen?"

Nancy nodded.

"Then you know that she worked at Roget's, the expensive jewelry store on Main Street," Mrs. Crown continued. "Karen was accused of stealing six of Roget's most valuable diamonds from their French marquis collection. Together the six diamonds were worth well over a million dollars. Five of the stolen diamonds have never been located, but because one of them was discovered in Karen's possession, she was found guilty of the theft."

Mrs. Crown added in a grim voice, "My daughter is currently serving a three-year term in the State Women's Correctional Institution."

Nancy was aware of the grief in Mrs. Crown's

eyes. "And you believe your daughter is innocent?" she asked gently.

Mrs. Crown replied firmly, "I *know* my daughter is innocent. She was framed for the theft. I received this anonymous note in the mail yesterday." She pulled a folded piece of paper from her pocket and handed it to Nancy.

Nancy carefully examined the blue stationery. The note had been handwritten in ink. It said:

Mrs. Crown,
I helped frame Karen for a crime that she did not commit. Forgive me.

The note was unsigned.

Nancy looked up and asked, "Mrs. Crown, do you mind if I keep this?"

Mrs. Crown nodded in agreement. "Another reason I need your help, Nancy, is because two days ago I received a threatening phone call. Then, yesterday morning, I received another one."

Nancy leaned forward. "What exactly did the caller say?"

Mrs. Crown nervously fingered the gold watch on her left wrist. "The caller warned me to stop my investigation, or I'd die." She gave a shudder. "The caller said the same thing both times."

"Have you been investigating the Roget robbery?" Nancy asked.

"Yes, I have," Monica Crown admitted. "The

7

case is officially closed, according to the police, but I don't want Karen to spend the next three years in prison. I've spent a great deal of time poking and prying into a lot of people's personal business. The real criminal evidently knows this, and he—or she—is afraid I might expose him."

"Do you have any idea at all who the calls were from?" Nancy asked.

"No. The caller's voice was very cleverly disguised through the use of some electronic device."

Nancy said firmly, "Mrs. Crown, if I'm going to help you find out who's really responsible for the Roget robbery, I think the first thing I should do is talk to your daughter."

The older woman nodded. "I agree. Anyway, I'd like you to meet Karen. I'm sure that once you do, you'll see that she couldn't possibly be involved in any kind of crime." Mrs. Crown hesitated. "Nancy, I'd feel more comfortable if you'd stay here until this whole thing is settled. I hate to admit it, but these threats on my life have really frightened me."

"That's a good idea," Nancy agreed quickly. "I'll move in this afternoon."

"Thank you, Nancy, but tomorrow morning will be fine." Mrs. Crown forced a weary smile. "I'll go over my notes with you and fill you in on all of the details of the case then."

Mrs. Crown looked at her watch and stood up. "I'm afraid I have to leave for an appointment now," she said. "But I'll see you tomorrow morning at, say, nine o'clock?"

Nancy followed Monica Crown out of the library and down the wide hall leading to the entryway. "Mrs. Crown, who knows that you've been investigating the Roget robbery?" Nancy asked as they walked down the hall to the door.

The author replied, "Well, I've talked to everyone at Roget's. Actually, I told them that the notes I've been taking and the questions I've been asking are material for my new book. In fact, once this case is solved and the real criminal is found, I do intend to write a book based on the case." She added, "My secretary, Madeline Simmons, and my publishers in New York know about the book. But only Madeline knows I've been trying to find the real criminal."

"Someone else knows, too," Nancy pointed out. "Your mysterious caller." Then she asked, "What about your household staff?"

"I employ a very small staff," Mrs. Crown said. "Just Mrs. Adams, who is my housekeeper and cook, and a part-time gardener. I've confided in Mrs. Adams. She's been with me for years." The author frowned. "And then there's Tony."

"Tony?" Nancy asked.

"Tony is Mrs. Adams's twenty-year-old son," Mrs. Crown explained. "He's lived here with his mother since he was a small boy. Tony does all sorts of odd jobs around my estate." Mrs. Crown sighed. "To be honest, Tony doesn't really earn his keep, but I haven't the heart to fire him because I care a great deal about his mother, Irene."

At the front door, Monica Crown and Nancy shook hands again. Nancy looked at the ring on Mrs. Crown's right hand. "That gold ring you're wearing—I've never seen one like it before."

Mrs. Crown laughed. "It *is* unique. My late husband had it custom-made for me after my first book was published. The book was called *The Case of the Cross-eyed Dragon.*" She held the ring out for Nancy's inspection. "That's what this is—a cross-eyed dragon."

Nancy looked more closely at the ring. "I see. And the crossed eyes are emeralds. It's really beautiful."

"Yes, it is." Monica Crown sighed. "Lawrence, my husband, was a wonderful man. I miss him. And now, with Karen in prison . . ."

"Don't worry, Mrs. Crown," replied Nancy. "She won't be in prison much longer—not if *I* can help it!"

At eight o'clock that night, Nancy was relaxing at the Pizza Palace with her two best friends, Bess Marvin and George Fayne. Although Bess and George were first cousins, the girls were complete opposites. Blond, blue-eyed Bess was slightly plump and very pretty. Her main interests in life were boys, clothes, and food. Brown-haired, brown-eyed George was tall, attractive,

10

and athletic. Despite their differences, the cousins were very close, not only to each other, but to Nancy as well.

Nancy had spent their first hour at the restaurant filling Bess and George in on her meeting with Mrs. Crown, and she had shown them the anonymous note. Over a third piece of cheese-and-pepperoni pizza, Bess declared dreamily, "Imagine, working for a famous celebrity like Monica Crown! I've read every book she's ever written."

"Well, I don't read as much as you two," George said, "but I definitely wouldn't miss a movie based on one of her books."

Bess rolled her eyes. "It's not the same thing at all," she informed her cousin. "Anyone can tell you that a book is always better than a movie. Right, Nancy?"

Nancy laughed good-naturedly. "You're not getting me into that old argument. I happen to like both."

It was well after eleven o'clock by the time they left the Pizza Palace. Nancy drove along with her fingers tapping against the steering wheel, keeping the beat to one of her favorite rock songs. Suddenly the radio went silent. After several seconds, the disk jockey came back on the air. "Sorry to interrupt Monday Night Top-Ten Countdown here on WRVH, but we've just received this special news bulletin. River Heights police have discovered the wreckage of a late-model green sports car at the bottom of Stone Canyon."

Unconsciously, Nancy, Bess, and George all strained to hear the disk jockey's next words. "The car is registered to famed mystery writer Monica Crown."

2

A Terrible Accident

"Mrs. Crown! I . . . I just can't believe it!" Nancy gasped.

Bess shuddered. "Those threats on her life must have been for real," she whispered.

"The accident happened in Stone Canyon," George said. "That's not too far from here."

Nancy nodded grimly. "Let's go," she said, turning the car in the direction of the hills just north of town. She stepped on the accelerator. The sound of sirens first alerted the girls that they were near the scene of the accident. As they rounded a sharp curve in the road, they saw half a dozen flashing lights ahead.

Nancy pulled the car over close to the embankment and switched off the engine. The three girls got out and walked to the site of the accident.

In the light of the full moon it was easy to

follow the path the car had taken as it had left the road, shot up over the dirt embankment, and plunged into the dark, deep ravine two hundred feet below.

Several police officers and ambulance attendants had already scrambled over the side of the cliff and were searching the area around the wreckage.

Bess shook her head. "No one could have lived through this."

Just then a paneled TV van drove up. A press car screeched to a halt behind the truck, and a young woman jumped out.

"Hey, look who's here," George said. "It's Allison Phillips, the On the Spot reporter for Channel Ten."

Nancy watched Allison Phillips run straight for the police officer in charge. A cameraman, following along a few feet behind Allison, balanced a video TV camera on his right shoulder. Nancy smiled a little as the aggressive young reporter pushed a microphone under the nose of the busy police officer.

Curious spectators were gathering to watch the grim scene below. At the fringe of the crowd, Nancy caught sight of Irene Adams. "Look"— she pointed—"that's Mrs. Adams, Mrs. Crown's housekeeper. I'm going to find out what she knows about this. I'll be right back."

Nancy made her way through a maze of police cars, an ambulance, and an assortment of other vehicles that were now parked by the cliff.

14

She watched Mrs. Adams walk slowly away from the crowd. The housekeeper leaned against the trunk of a large tree for support.

"Mrs. Adams?" Nancy called out.

Mrs. Adams's eyes were wide with fear. She stared vacantly as Nancy approached.

"Mrs. Adams," Nancy repeated. "I'm Nancy Drew. I met you at Mrs. Crown's home earlier today."

It took a few minutes for Nancy's words to register. Finally, Mrs. Adams nodded. "Oh, yes. . . . I remember now. . . ." The housekeeper's words trailed off and she broke into uncontrollable sobs. "This is so terrible. . . . I've worked for Mrs. Crown for over twenty years. She's such a fine woman. I can't believe she's dead," Mrs. Adams said in a choking voice.

Nancy spoke gently to the older woman. "Don't give up hope, Mrs. Adams. They haven't found a body yet. Is it possible," Nancy asked, "that someone else was driving Mrs. Crown's car?"

"No," Mrs. Adams replied. "I saw Mrs. Crown leave in the car at around five o'clock this afternoon. She was alone."

Nancy nodded. "She told me she had an appointment." Then she added, "But she left the house nearly seven hours ago. I wonder where she was during all that time." Nancy spoke more to herself than to the housekeeper. "Did she tell you where she was going or who she was meeting?"

15

"No. She just told me not to wait up for her. She said she might be out quite late." Mrs. Adams wrapped her arms around herself in an effort to control her trembling body. "I only hope that Tony . . ." She choked on a sob.

"Your son?" Nancy asked quickly. "What about him?"

"I only hope that he wasn't involved with this accident."

Nancy wondered why Mrs. Adams would be worried about that, but she decided not to say anything. She didn't want to add to the woman's distress.

A young man wandered over to them. His dirty-blond hair was cut in an outrageous style, and he was wearing torn jeans and a black leather jacket. "They still haven't found the old lady's body," he announced in a casual voice.

He pushed his hands inside his jean pockets. "It's too bad about the car. Mrs. C. let me drive it to the gas station for a fill-up this morning. What a great ride!"

"Tony!" Mrs. Adams looked embarrassed. "Is that all you can think about—the *car*? Mrs. Crown might be dead!" Mrs. Adams walked away in disgust. Tony gave a careless shrug and sauntered off.

Nancy looked thoughtfully at Tony. Then she headed back across the road toward Bess and George. But before she could reach her friends, Allison Phillips rushed up to her, followed by a

16

cameraman and another young man holding a portable klieg light. Nancy blinked in the glare of the light.

Nancy tried to walk away, but Allison Phillips grabbed her arm and turned her around so that they were both facing the camera. "Ladies and gentlemen," Allison said, "I'm standing here with Nancy Drew, River Heights's best-known detective. Nancy, what can you tell us about the horrible accident that has happened tonight? Are you going to investigate the case?" She shoved the microphone in Nancy's face.

"Look, Ms. Phillips, if you don't mind, I'd rather not be interviewed right now," Nancy replied flatly. She pulled her arm away from Allison Phillips's grasp and began to walk away.

"But my viewers want to know," Allison protested, as she hurried after Nancy. "Don't you think they have a right to know why you're here?"

Nancy ignored Allison's question. Instead she asked, "Did you get any information about the accident from the police?"

The reporter smiled and shook her head. "Any information I have, you can learn all about on the Channel Ten news report," Allison replied sweetly. She turned to the cameraman and said, "I wish we knew a little more about what Mrs. Crown has been up to lately. She's so reclusive, no one in River Heights has seen her since her daughter's trial months ago."

Nancy couldn't resist saying, "I saw her today."

"What!" the reporter exclaimed. "Where did you see her?"

"At her home," Nancy replied calmly.

Allison's eyebrows shot up. She looked at Nancy and smiled slyly. "So you *are* investigating something. What is it?" she asked.

Nancy shook her head. "I'm not telling you anything, Ms. Phillips." Nancy smiled to herself as she joined Bess and George.

Another half hour passed before the police officer in charge informed everyone that rescuers were having a difficult time searching through the dense foliage at the bottom of the ravine. No body had been found. Most of the officers were being sent home. Two search teams would continue working throughout the night. The policeman urged the crowd to leave.

Nancy was both relieved and puzzled that a body hadn't been found. She dropped Bess and George off at their respective homes and returned to her own home for the night.

At ten o'clock the next morning, Nancy entered her father's office. "Here are those papers you asked me to bring you," she said, placing a bulging manila envelope on Mr. Drew's desk.

"I listened to the radio on the way over," she added. "The police still haven't found a body near the site of the wreck." Nancy's eyes were filled with concern. "It's hard to believe that

Mrs. Crown probably died in the accident last night."

Carson Drew was thoughtful. He brushed a hand over his dark hair, which was just beginning to show traces of gray. "I know how you feel. She seemed like a special lady."

"Alive or dead, I'm not going to let her down," Nancy declared. "I'm starting work on this case today. I thought I'd begin by having a look around Mrs. Crown's library. When I was there yesterday, I noticed that her desk was covered with papers. Maybe I can find a clue among some of her notes."

"My firm is as concerned about Monica Crown's disappearance as you are, Nancy. She's a very important client. If I can help in any way, let me know."

Nancy gave her father a grateful smile. "Thanks, Dad. I know I can always count on you."

Twenty minutes later, Nancy was ringing the doorbell of Mrs. Crown's house. A red-eyed Mrs. Adams showed Nancy into the library. Nancy headed straight for the desk and sat down in the big leather chair behind it.

Mrs. Adams said nervously, "Well, I have a few things to attend to upstairs. Will you be all right here alone?"

"I'll be fine, Mrs. Adams," Nancy said. "Thank you."

When the housekeeper had left, Nancy combed the top of the desk thoroughly, searching for clues. Most of the papers were bank and business correspondence. A large stack of fan letters stood on the right side of the desk. Next to the pile of letters was a photograph of a young woman. Karen Crown, Nancy guessed. Beside the photo was a calendar. Nancy flipped through the pages, but she didn't find anything revealing. The page with yesterday's date was completely blank. Next Nancy checked all the desk drawers. Inside the lower left drawer were several handwritten pages that looked to Nancy like an outline for some future mystery that Mrs. Crown was planning.

Nancy was about to read the outline when the grandfather clock in the library began to strike the hour. She glanced at her watch and saw that it was noon. Nancy carefully folded the pages and tucked them inside her shoulder bag.

She said a hurried goodbye to Mrs. Adams and dashed to her car. It was time to have a talk with Karen Crown.

The drive to the State Women's Correctional Institution took nearly two hours. The prison had only minimum security, but Nancy had to stop at the security desk and submit to a brief search before she was allowed to enter.

She waited for Karen Crown inside a bare room that contained a steel table and two folding chairs. There was no window. The only light came from a single one-hundred-watt bulb that glared from the ceiling. Even though she was wearing a leather jacket, Nancy felt the chill of the cement walls around her.

The green steel door opened. Karen Crown was led inside by a female guard. The guard announced bluntly, "You have fifteen minutes. I'll be just outside."

The door closed with a bang. Karen let out a sigh, and she sank weakly into one of the chairs. "You're Nancy Drew?" she asked in a shaky voice.

Nancy felt a rush of pity as she thought of the photograph she'd seen in Mrs. Crown's library. In that photograph Karen had worn a dazzling smile. With her silky blond hair and sparkling blue eyes, she had been a beautiful young woman.

Now, after a few months in prison, Karen Crown's hair had become limp, and she had dark circles under her eyes. She propped her elbows on the table and rested her head between her hands. She seemed exhausted and much older than her twenty-five years.

"Karen, I'm here because I want to help you," Nancy said.

A faint smile briefly crossed Karen's pale face. "I hope you can help me, Nancy. I spoke to my mother on the phone yesterday. She told me she had just asked you to help us."

"Have you spoken to your mother since then?" Nancy asked.

Karen shook her head.

Nancy hesitated. Karen certainly didn't need

any more problems. She asked as gently as she could, "Have you heard about last night's accident?"

Karen's eyes filled with tears. "Yes, I was told this morning." She swallowed hard, fighting to control her quavering voice. "I can't believe that my mother's really dead. . . ."

Nancy said quickly, "Until they find her body, there's always hope, Karen."

Karen nodded and wiped the tears away from her cheeks. "The last thing my mother said to me was that she was working hard to have my name cleared and that I'd be out of here soon."

Nancy leaned across the table toward Karen. "Let's start at the beginning," she said. "I'd like you to tell me about the robbery."

Karen shook her head. "There's not much to tell. It happened on a Friday night, about an hour after I had left Roget's. The next morning Roget's was closed to the public. The store was swarming with police officers. I must have been questioned by at least a dozen people that morning; it was a nightmare. They had no reason to suspect me, other than the fact that I had no alibi for my whereabouts the night before."

"Where were you the night of the robbery?" Nancy asked.

"I was supposed to meet Larry—Larry Holtz, my fiancé," Karen explained, "in front of a theater in Petersville. We were planning to see a movie and then go out for a late dinner. I waited outside the theater for about forty-five minutes, but Larry never showed up. By that time it had started to rain, so I bought a ticket and went inside."

"Were there any witnesses, anyone who remembered seeing you outside the theater?" Nancy wanted to know.

"No," Karen replied, "that was the problem. I had no way of proving where I was when Roget's diamonds were stolen."

"What happened to Larry?"

"His car had broken down. He was stranded eighteen miles from the closest town. I was back home before he was able to get in touch with me."

"Do you live with your mother?" asked Nancy.

"Yes, I live in a small apartment over the garage."

Nancy started jotting down notes. "Can you tell me about your fiancé?"

Karen's expression softened, and she smiled for the first time. She said warmly, "Larry is just a year older than I am. He's a very successful gem dealer. The missing diamonds had been brought to Roget's by Larry. He wanted Tom Owens to cut them."

"Who is Tom Owens?" Nancy asked.

"Tom Owens is a well-known stonecutter. Cutting precious stones requires a great deal of skill. Although Tom lives in River Heights, he's worked for the Roget's chain all over the United States. He is"—Karen paused—"or was one of the industry's most skilled stonecutters."

Nancy looked up from her notepad. "What do you mean, 'was'? Doesn't he cut stones any-more?"

"No, he was recently forced to retire. He has some kind of problem with his hands and can't work any longer."

Nancy said, "Your mother told me the police were sure you were guilty when they searched your apartment and found one of the missing diamonds."

Karen's lips were set in a straight, tight line. "That diamond was planted in my bedroom dresser. I was set up to take the blame for the robbery."

"Let's go back to the time just before you left Roget's," Nancy suggested. "Did anybody there do or say anything that seemed suspicious?"

Karen thought for a minute. Then she shook her head. "No, everybody seemed pretty nor-mal." She added, "The only weird thing that happened was that, later, Al Morris, the security guard, was drugged. I found out about it the next day. He was unconscious during the robbery."

"Drugged!" Nancy exclaimed. "But how?"

Karen shrugged helplessly. "I don't know. It couldn't have been the coffee. I made a fresh pot before I left Roget's at six o'clock. I even drank a cup just before I left for my date with Larry."

"Maybe the cup Al Morris drank was from another pot of coffee," Nancy suggested.

"No, that's impossible," replied Karen. "We had only one pot in the lounge."

"Anyone at Roget's could have substituted coffee pots with a little planning," Nancy pointed out. "Or someone could have slipped the drug into Al Morris's cup directly." Then she asked, "Is there some way I can get in touch with Larry? I'd like to talk to him, too."

"He'll be here tomorrow," Karen said softly. "He drives all the way up here once a week. I'll tell him to get in touch with you."

The green steel door opened. "Time's up, ladies," the guard announced.

"Nancy?"

Nancy paused and looked at Karen. The young woman was gazing at her with a hopeful expression. "Larry and I were supposed to be married over the Thanksgiving holiday. That's only a little over a month away. Do you think there's any way that can still happen?"

Nancy reached out and gave Karen's arm a reassuring squeeze. "I don't know, Karen, but I promise I'll do everything I can."

As Nancy headed out the door, Karen suddenly cried out, "Nancy, wait!"

"What is it?" Nancy said, turning around.

"I forgot to give you a copy of the first two chapters of Mother's new book. Maybe you can find some clues in it." She handed Nancy a manila folder.

"Have you read the chapters?" Nancy asked Karen.

The young woman shook her head. "Not yet. I just received it today."

25

Nancy took the folder and promised Karen she would read the chapters very carefully.

Twenty minutes later Nancy was speeding along the highway back toward River Heights. She glanced at the folder on the seat beside her. She was so anxious to read what Mrs. Crown had written that she pulled into the first roadside restaurant parking lot she could find.

Nancy hadn't eaten since breakfast, and she was starving. She found a comfortable booth in the small diner and ordered her meal.

While she waited for her food, she pulled the typewritten pages from the manila folder. Mrs. Crown's new mystery still didn't have a title. Nancy hadn't even completed the first paragraph when she was startled by a scream coming from the main entrance to the diner. She was suddenly aware of smoke and the crackling sound of a fire out of control!

3

The First Warning

The small restaurant was filled with panic as customers left their tables and raced to the rear exit.

A mother with three young children was headed toward the exit. The youngest child stumbled and fell. Nancy quickly scooped the little girl up in her arms.

A waitress used the plastic tray she was carrying to break the glass to the fire extinguisher. Within a matter of minutes the fire was under control, and the restaurant employees urged customers to return to their seats. Nancy handed the small, frightened child over to her mother and returned to her corner booth. Her jacket and purse were where she had left them, but the chapters to Mrs. Crown's book were missing!

By this time the diner was filled with firefighters. Nancy darted out the rear door and raced around to the parking lot in front of the diner. She spotted a white sedan speeding out of the lot and onto the highway. The driver of the car was obviously in a great hurry, but Nancy reasoned that might just be a coincidence. She sighed and went back into the restaurant. She gave the area around her booth a final inspection. After questioning several customers and her waitress, Nancy decided that the chapters had been stolen.

Later that evening Nancy was in the kitchen helping to get dinner ready. "It's so embarrassing," she said to Hannah. "I'm supposed to be a detective, and I let someone steal those pages right from under my nose."

"Don't be so hard on yourself, Nancy," Hannah said sympathetically. "I'm sure the same thing could have happened to anyone."

Nancy sighed. She removed a tray of Hannah's piping hot rolls from the oven and placed them in a serving basket.

Just then Carson Drew stepped into the kitchen. He breathed in deeply. "Everything smells wonderful," he said, grinning at Hannah. To Nancy he said, "You look a little tired, honey. Is anything wrong?"

Nancy reached up and gave her father a light kiss on the cheek. "I'm glad you're home, Dad. I've got a lot to tell you."

During dinner Nancy filled her father in on all

the details of the day. Her blue eyes darkened as she recalled her visit to Karen Crown at the prison. "It's really awful there, Dad. Karen seemed so depressed and lonely. I don't think she can stand being in prison much longer."

Nancy paused, her fork in midair, and said thoughtfully, "It must be horrible enough being locked up in a place like that if you're guilty, but if you're innocent . . ." She set her fork down. She said in a determined voice, "I'm going to get Karen out of there."

"I'm sure you will, Nancy," replied her father. "Just don't get impatient. It could take some time to settle this case. It sounds to me as if at least two people are involved in the Roget's robbery." Mr. Drew reached for a second portion of salmon. "Mrs. Crown told you that she received calls threatening her life. She also received a note telling her Karen was innocent. That sounds like two people to me. One afraid of getting caught, and the other feeling guilty about sending an innocent person to jail."

"If only I'd caught a glimpse of whoever stole those pages today."

"Yes, it's too bad about that," her father agreed.

"Well, anyway, I'm going to start concentrating on interviewing some of the people who work at Roget's."

Nancy and Carson Drew were just finishing dessert when the phone rang.

Hannah called from the kitchen. "Nancy, it's for you."

"Thanks, Hannah," Nancy called back. "I'll take it in the den." Nancy sat down behind her father's mahogany desk. Before picking up the phone, she automatically reached for a pen.

The voice on the other end of the phone seemed nervous and in somewhat of a hurry. "Hello, Miss Drew? My name is Paul Reese. I got your name from Karen Crown. She's my cousin. Monica Crown is my aunt. I'd like to talk to you about my aunt's disappearance."

"Of course," Nancy replied eagerly. "Do you know anything about Mrs. Crown's accident?"

Paul Reese hesitated before answering. "I can't talk right now, but I have some information that might be helpful. I'm a student at Emerson College. Can you meet me here at the Campus Coffee Shop?"

"Yes, I can," Nancy replied. "I'll be there at eleven o'clock tomorrow morning."

Nancy's boyfriend, Ned Nickerson, was a student at Emerson College. As soon as Paul Reese hung up, Nancy dialed Ned's fraternity house. She was told that Ned was out. Nancy left a message asking Ned if he'd be free to have lunch with her in the college cafeteria at noon the next day.

The drive to Emerson College was pleasant. Nancy enjoyed the scenic beauty of the countryside, bright with the red, orange, and gold colors of autumn.

When Nancy reached the college, she parked in the visitors' parking lot and walked across the campus toward the coffee shop. As she stepped inside the building, she checked her watch. Ten fifty-five exactly. Nancy always liked to be a few minutes early for appointments.

The coffee shop was fairly empty. Nancy sat at a table near the door, ordered a soda, and waited for Paul Reese.

At eleven-fifteen, a tall, thin young man with red hair stepped into the coffee shop. He glanced around the restaurant.

Nancy said, "Excuse me, but are you Paul Reese?"

Paul looked at Nancy in surprise. "Yeah, but . . . you can't be . . . I mean, are you Nancy Drew?"

"Yes," Nancy replied with a smile. She stood up and held out her hand.

Paul wordlessly shook her hand. Then he sat down on a chair next to Nancy, staring at her out of thick horned-rimmed glasses that magnified his pale green eyes. It didn't take Nancy long to decide that he was definitely rude.

"How old are you anyway?" he demanded angrily.

"I'm eighteen," Nancy replied.

"I don't believe it! Now I know Aunt Monica really lost all her marbles!"

"Is this your way of telling me that you think I'm too young to be a detective?" Nancy inquired politely.

"Let's face it," Paul said. "You can't have had much experience."

"Actually, I've solved a number of cases," Nancy replied matter-of-factly. "Ability has nothing to do with how old you are."

Unconvinced, Paul continued to scowl at Nancy. She reached in her purse for a pen and notebook. "You told me on the phone you had some information about your aunt."

"I know she was writing a book based on the Roget's robbery."

Nancy placed her pen on top of her notebook and said, "Yes, I know that."

Paul seemed surprised. "She told you about the book?"

"She didn't tell me its contents, only that she hoped that the book she was working on might expose the thief."

"So that's why she was snooping around Roget's," Paul said slowly. He added, "My father was very annoyed that she kept showing up there. He's the manager of Roget's."

"Frederick Reese is your father?" Nancy asked in surprise.

Paul nodded.

"I just talked to his secretary this morning," Nancy said. "I made an appointment to speak to him tomorrow." She paused. "It's funny that no one has mentioned that he's related to Mrs. Crown."

"What do you mean?" Paul stared down at Nancy. His expression was anything but friendly. "Who have you been talking to anyway?"

"So far I've only talked to your aunt and to Karen."

"Karen!" Paul gave a snort of contempt. "My jailbird cousin. She'd say anything to get out of prison."

Nancy ignored Paul's words and turned the conversation back to Frederick Reese. "Exactly how are your father and Mrs. Crown related?"

"They're brother and sister," Paul replied. Then he added in a threatening tone, "Don't try to pin anything on my father."

Nancy's eyes widened. "I have no reason to suspect your father of anything. But since he is the manager of Roget's, I thought it was only logical to talk to him."

"He doesn't know anything about Aunt Monica's accident," Paul said hotly. "Why don't you leave him alone?"

Nancy tossed the pen and notebook back inside her purse. She pulled the leather strap of the bag over her shoulder and walked to the door. Only Nancy's flashing eyes betrayed her anger. "Do you mind telling me why you wanted me to drive out here? It's obvious that you don't have anything helpful to tell me about your aunt or her disappearance."

"I can tell you that a lot of people stand to benefit from her death," Paul blurted out.

Nancy paused, her hand on the doorknob. "What do you mean?"

Paul's whole attitude changed. He looked away from Nancy and mumbled, "I mean that my aunt was a very rich woman."

Nancy raised her eyebrows. "Are you suggesting that one of her heirs might be responsible for her disappearance?"

Paul shrugged. "It's possible."

Nancy looked at Paul closely. She said slowly, "Does that make you a possible suspect? Or your father?"

Paul Reese banged his fist on the table. "I did not harm my aunt! And neither did my father! I just wish that you or the police or somebody would hurry up and find her body."

"What makes you so sure she's dead?"

"Come on," Paul sneered, "even a teenage detective must have brains enough to figure out that people don't survive a drop from a two-hundred-foot-high cliff!"

With these words, Paul got up and marched out of the coffee shop.

Nancy sat in the coffee shop for a few minutes thinking about her conversation with Paul Reese. Then she paid her bill and left to meet Ned.

The walk from the Campus Coffee Shop to the cafeteria only took a few minutes. Nancy was excited at the prospect of seeing Ned. She hoped that he had gotten her message.

"Nancy!"

Nancy whirled in the direction of Ned's voice. She saw the tall, athletic young man bound down the steps of the science building toward her. He gave her a hug and said, "It's great to see you."

"It's great to see you, too," Nancy said with a smile.

Ned linked Nancy's arm through his as they headed for the cafeteria. "What brings you to Emerson anyway?"

Nancy said teasingly, "What makes you think I didn't drive out here just to see my favorite guy?"

Ned laughed. "That would be nice, but something tells me that you're combining business with pleasure."

Over a leisurely lunch, Nancy told Ned all about the Crown case, up to her conversation with Paul Reese. After she had finished, Ned commented, "It sounds as if Paul wants his aunt to be proven dead."

"That was the feeling I got, too," Nancy said. "If there's no body, a will can be held up for years. Paul seems to be interested in his aunt's money."

As they left the cafeteria, Ned said, "I've got a two o'clock class. It's on the other side of the campus, so I've got to get moving. I'll see you on Saturday. Don't forget my parents are expecting us at the lake for the day."

Nancy smiled. "Are you kidding? I've been looking forward to it ever since you· called last week to invite me."

As Nancy walked to her car, she heard the squeal of tires behind her. Turning, she watched a white sedan speed from the parking lot and down one of the usually quiet college streets. When she reached her sportscar, Nancy saw that the door on the driver's side was slightly open. She was positive that she'd locked it. With a puzzled frown, she pulled the door open.

Spread all over the driver's seat was a Polaroid snapshot ripped to shreds! When Nancy fit the pieces together, she saw that it was a picture of her taken with Ned when they had met outside the science building.

Then Nancy noticed a note that had fallen on the floor. Scribbled in black ink were the words: "If you want to stay in one piece, drop the Crown case!"

4

Followed!

Nancy glanced around quickly. There was no one in sight. "Whoever you are," she spoke under her breath, "if you're trying to scare me off . . . forget it!"

Less than ten minutes after leaving Emerson College, Nancy became aware of a car following her. She was sure it was the same white sedan that had peeled out of the college parking lot seconds before she had discovered the torn photograph. She recalled the white sedan she'd seen leaving the roadside diner shortly after she'd discovered that the pages of Mrs. Crown's book were missing. Someone was keeping very close tabs on her whereabouts!

Nancy stepped harder on the accelerator. The little sportscar surged forward. The car behind her immediately picked up speed. Nancy decided to slow down in the hope that she could draw the sedan close enough to see who was behind the wheel, but it remained a safe distance behind. Then she noticed that the windows of the sedan were tinted black.

"This is ridiculous," Nancy said aloud. No matter how close she got to the other car, it would be impossible to see inside. She decided to wait until she reached the next town before making a move to lose the unwelcome tail.

When she reached the town of Petersville, Nancy made a sudden turn off the main highway onto one of the smaller city streets. She whipped the car around a maze of city blocks. When she left Petersville she was headed back to River Heights on another route.

Nancy grinned triumphantly into the rearview mirror. The white sedan was nowhere in sight. The alternate route would take slightly longer, but at least she'd be traveling without "company."

The next morning Nancy dressed with care for her appointment at Roget's, the most exclusive jewelry store in town. Customers usually had to make an appointment just to look at some of the more precious stones in their collection.

As she headed downstairs, Hannah called out, "Nancy, you'd better take a coat. There's a real chill in the air today."

Nancy glanced out the window. The October weather was turning cooler with each passing day. The sky was gray and overcast. "Good idea,

Hannah. Actually, it looks like it's going to pour any minute." Nancy took a lined trenchcoat from the hall closet and tossed it over her arm. Hannah came into the hall.

"I can't stop worrying about that torn photograph," she said in a concerned voice. "Someone would have to be crazy to tear up a picture and leave a note like that."

"I don't think so, Hannah," Nancy said, trying to be reassuring. "Someone just wanted to frighten me."

"Well, whoever it is certainly managed to frighten *me.*" She reached out and patted Nancy's shoulder. "Please, dear, promise me you'll be careful."

Nancy smiled. "I will, Hannah. I promise."

Twenty minutes later, Nancy pulled into George's driveway. The front door opened, and George made a dash for the car. A light rain had started to fall. On the drive into town Nancy told her all about what had happened on her trip to Emerson. When Nancy had finished, George said, "I think the torn picture and the threatening note are easy to understand."

"Oh?" Nancy was curious to hear George's explanation.

"I figure that it was done by some heartbroken Emerson student who is secretly in love with Ned. When she got a look at you, she realized she'd never stand a chance with the man of her dreams . . . unless she could scare you off."

Nancy chuckled. Then in a serious voice she

said, "That torn photograph didn't really scare me, but it does convince me that someone means business. And the sooner I find out who that someone is, the better!"

For the rest of their ride, Nancy and George's conversation was centered on the Crown case.

The entrance to Roget's was very distinctive. A red-striped awning hung high above the storefront, and there was a red-carpeted walk leading up to the door.

Nancy and George were greeted by a friendly guard at the door. He held the barred steel gates open for the girls. Nancy hesitated, then she said, "Excuse me, but I see by your name tag that you're Al Morris."

Al Morris was a heavyset, jolly-looking man in his early sixties. He grinned at Nancy and said, "Yes, I am. How can I help you young ladies?"

"My name is Nancy Drew. I'm here to ask some questions about the robbery that took place last May. I understand you were on duty that night."

The security guard's grin faded. He seemed immediately cautious. "Yes, I was on duty that night. May I ask, miss, does Mr. Reese know you're here to investigate the diamond robbery?"

"Yes, he does," Nancy replied. "When I made the appointment, I told his secretary what I wanted to talk to him about."

Al Morris seemed to relax a little. He shrugged. "Well, I can't be very helpful. I was unconscious during the whole thing. The police lab found traces of a sleeping powder in the coffee pot. I had had two or three cups right after I came on duty that night."

Nancy's eyes carefully studied Al Morris's face as she spoke her next words. "I spoke to Karen Crown. She says she made a pot of coffee before leaving at six o'clock that night. She even drank a cup from that pot. She swears it wasn't drugged when she left Roget's."

Al Morris's gray eyes shifted from Nancy to George. He said, "Look, I always liked Miss Crown. I could never believe she was the thief. Even after she was arrested, I figured she'd get off." Al shrugged. "I'm sorry, I don't know how the drugs got into that pot of coffee or who put them there. All I know is that I was definitely drugged."

Nancy thanked the guard, and she and George stepped into the shop. Walking between rows of enclosed glass cases, Nancy and George couldn't help but admire all the expensive jewelry surrounding them.

"Oh, wow," George whispered, stopping by one of the cases. "What I would give for that gorgeous emerald ring."

Nancy's eyes fell on the price tag, which had been accidentally turned over. "It's a real bargain, George," Nancy whispered back. "Only fourteen thousand dollars!"

The girls were led into Frederick Reese's office by his secretary. She introduced Nancy and

George to Mr. Reese. Then she left the office, closing the door behind her.

Nancy and George sat down in the matching Victorian chairs that faced Frederick Reese's large antique desk. Frederick Reese, Nancy noted, was an older version of his son. He was slightly taller and heavier than Paul, but he had the same pale green eyes that stared out from behind thick horn-rimmed glasses.

Mr. Reese leaned forward. With an arrogant smile he said, "I really don't know what you think you can learn from me about the robbery. I've told the police everything I know. I testified at the trial. I've been interviewed by newspaper and TV reporters." Frederick Reese stopped smiling. His voice began to rise in anger. "Insurance investigators have been on my back. Frankly, I'm fed up with the whole business."

"Mr. Reese," Nancy purposely spoke in a low voice in an effort to calm the store manager, "do you believe Karen Crown is guilty?"

Frederick Reese looked at Nancy thoughtfully. Then he shook his head sadly. "My own sister's child. She's a lovely girl. I didn't want to believe that she had anything to do with it, but facts are facts. One of the stolen diamonds was found in her apartment."

Nancy's next question surprised George, who had been silently but intently studying Mr. Reese. "Assuming that Karen is guilty, do you believe she pulled off the diamond robbery by herself?"

"No." Frederick Reese's reply was immediate. "I've always thought that fiancé of hers, Larry Holtz, was involved."

"Do you have any reason to suspect him?" Nancy inquired.

The store manager shrugged. "Just call it a hunch, but I did notice that right after the robbery, Holtz bought himself a very expensive new car."

Nancy jotted down this information in her notebook. "What can you tell me about Tom Owens?"

"He was one of the finest stonecutters in America. Before his hands started to go, he received calls from gem dealers around the world."

Nancy remembered that Karen had also mentioned Tom Owens's hands. "I don't understand. What happened to his hands?"

"Arthritis," Mr. Reese replied. There was a genuine note of sympathy in his voice. "Tom is still a fairly young man. To see a brilliant career come to an end for someone his age is a real tragedy."

"Then Mr. Owens no longer works here?"

"No, I was forced to ask him to resign. He retired from the business a few days after the robbery."

"I'd like to talk to Mr. Owens," Nancy said. "Can you give me his address?"

Mr. Reese nodded. He quickly jotted down the address and phone number on a piece of paper and handed the paper to Nancy.

"Now what?" George asked, as she and Nancy headed back to Nancy's car. "A visit to Tom Owens?"

"Right," Nancy replied. "It's time to get his side of the story."

On the way to Tom Owens's house, the October storm began in earnest. The rain seemed to come down in buckets. At one point Nancy was forced to creep along the highway at fifteen miles an hour.

Tom Owens lived in a rural section of River Heights. Each house was located at least half a mile from its closest neighbor. In the blinding rain, George was just able to make out the name on the mailbox next to the road. "This is it."

Nancy turned into a gravel driveway. At the end stood a red barnlike house. Nancy parked as close to the house as possible. Together, she and George made a dash through the rain to the shelter of the front porch.

Nancy used the brass knocker in the center of the door. On the second knock, the door opened.

Tom Owens didn't wait to ask his callers their names. Instead, he opened the door wide and invited them inside. The living room was cozy and warm. He motioned his guests over to the fireplace. After he had taken their coats, the girls reached out toward the warmth of the blazing fire.

Tom Owens was not much taller than George, who was five feet eight inches. With his slender but muscular build, dark hair, and black eyes, both girls were aware of his good looks.

He silently studied both girls before he said, "You must be Nancy Drew, and if I'm not mistaken," he said with a smile for George, "you're George Fayne."

"But . . . how . . ." George stammered.

"Let me guess," Nancy said, returning his smile. "Mr. Reese called to tell you that we wanted to talk to you."

"Very deductive reasoning," Tom Owens teased. "It's easy to see why you're such a successful detective."

Nancy laughed and sat down on the couch next to George. "I hope we're not interrupting, Mr. Owens. I suppose we should have called ahead ourselves. We just thought we'd take the chance you might be in."

"Call me Tom. And you're welcome to ask me any questions, although I don't think I can give you any helpful information—except to say that I'm certain the robbery was an inside job."

"What makes you so sure?" George asked.

"First of all, someone knew the combination to the alarm system. The alarm never went off. Second, only a Roget's employee could have had access to the coffee pot that drugged Al Morris. Finally, someone had to have inside knowledge about the exact time those particular diamonds were going to be at Roget's."

Tom Owens leaned against the fireplace mantel. "I've always believed that Karen Crown was framed. It's a real shame. If the thief was going to frame anybody, I don't know why he didn't frame Reese's son. He seems like the perfect person. He's always sponging money off people, his father included."

Nancy nodded thoughtfully. "He was very interested in finding out whether Mrs. Crown was alive or dead," she told Tom Owens.

"Have you met Paul?" Tom asked.

"Only once, briefly," Nancy replied. She added, "You aren't the only person to believe in Karen. Her mother recently received an anonymous note stating that Karen was innocent."

Tom Owens's dark eyes were curious. "Really? Did it say anything else?"

"No, unfortunately it didn't."

"The diamonds were worth nearly a million dollars," Tom informed the girls. "Almost anyone could use that kind of money—especially Frederick. He's had a lot of financial troubles lately."

"I'm surprised," George said. "Roget's seems to be prosperous."

"Oh, it is," Tom said. "But Frederick Reese has made some very unwise personal investments. He's lost a great deal of money on them."

"Mr. Reese seemed very fond of you," Nancy said. "He was very sorry that you had to retire at such an early age."

Tom replied bitterly, "Yes . . . well, he's not the only one." He held up his hands. They were just beginning to show signs of becoming abnormally curved and stiff. "I'm only thirty-eight years old. I should have been able to work for another thirty years."

"I'm very sorry, Tom," Nancy said gently.

Tom forced a smile. "That's okay. There are worse handicaps. I'm learning to live with it. Anyway, I've gone into business for myself. I'm a gemstone consultant. I advise stores on what kind of stones to buy. It keeps me busy."

After Nancy and George left Tom Owens they headed back to town where they met Bess for lunch at the Delight Bite Restaurant. They told Bess all about their meeting with Tom Owens.

"Is he really as good-looking as George says?" Bess asked Nancy.

"Forget it, Bess," Nancy said with a laugh. "Tom Owens is much too old for you."

Bess faked a sad sigh. "Too bad. So far Tom Owens sounds like the most interesting person connected with the Crown case."

George and Nancy exchanged looks. George said to Bess, "Just because he's the best-looking doesn't mean he's the most interesting."

Bess loved mysteries when they came safely wrapped up in books, but she wasn't crazy about Nancy's real-life mysteries or anything that hinted at being even remotely dangerous. However, she was naturally curious. "So, what's going on with this case anyway? I heard on the radio this morning that the police have stopped looking in Stone Canyon for Mrs. Crown's body. Do you think that means she survived the wreck? But how could she? And if she isn't dead, where is she?"

"I don't know," Nancy said, shrugging her shoulders helplessly. "I'm just as baffled as you are."

Just then, the waitress stopped by their table to see if the girls needed anything else. Bess didn't hesitate. "Yes, what do you have for dessert?"

Nancy and George looked at each other and smiled. Although Bess frequently complained about her extra five pounds, she was never able to turn down a dessert.

"Why don't we have dessert at my house," Nancy suggested. "I know for a fact that Hannah made a double-chocolate cake this morning."

"Sounds good to me," said Bess.

The storm was still raging as Nancy pulled into the driveway of her house. The three girls ran across the yard. "Nancy, the back door is wide open!" George yelled.

"Hannah?" Nancy called out as she entered the kitchen. Bess and George followed. "Hannah?" Nancy called again. "Are you here?"

There was no answer. The girls filed into the dining room. Nancy tossed her purse on the table and called the housekeeper's name once again. But this time there was a sense of urgency in her voice.

The girls rushed into the living room. There was no sign of Hannah. Nancy heard the sound of breaking glass. "The den!" she shouted. "Quick!"

Nancy ran into the den. There, torrents of rain were being blown across the room through an open window. A crystal vase which had stood on a table by the window lay in a million pieces on the floor.

As Nancy made a dash toward the window, she stumbled over her father's body. "Dad!" she screamed.

5

Break-in

"Dad!" Nancy knelt beside her father. She gently touched the back of Carson Drew's head. A
large lump had already started to form. Mr. Drew
groaned. His eyes slowly opened. He blinked
several times in an effort to bring his daughter's
frightened face into focus. "Dad," Nancy spoke
softly, "are you all right?"

Carson Drew winced with pain as he gingerly
touched the back of his head. With Nancy and
George's help he sat up. Together they managed
to get him to the closest chair.

Bess, who had been petrified at seeing Mr.
Drew unconscious, recovered from her initial
shock. Now aware of the rain still whipping into
the room, she hurriedly closed the window.

"Dad, what happened?" Nancy asked.

"I'm not sure," Mr. Drew replied. "I came
home from the office early. Hannah was out.

When I came in here, I noticed the open window. I started toward it when suddenly I was hit from behind. I think someone was searching through my desk."

Nancy said, "Whoever it was left in a big hurry out the kitchen door. It was wide open when we got here, and I guess the intruder came in through this window."

"I wonder where Han—" Before Nancy could finish her sentence, Hannah Gruen appeared in the doorway.

"Oh, no," she gasped when she saw Carson Drew. "What's happened?"

"I'm all right," Mr. Drew quickly assured her. "I was attacked by a burglar."

"That explains the phone call," Hannah said. She went to Carson Drew's side and inspected the lump on his head. Then she looked at Nancy. "About half an hour ago I received a call telling me that your car had broken down. The caller said you wanted me to pick you up at Hunter's Gas Station. When I got there no one knew anything about your car, so I waited awhile and then came back here."

"That was a trick to get you out of the house," Nancy said.

"The voice on the phone, Hannah," George asked, "did you recognize it?"

"No," Hannah replied. "It was a very bad connection, due to the storm, I suppose. I could hardly make out what the caller was saying. I'm not even sure if the voice was male or female."

"I wonder what the burglar was looking for." Nancy glanced through the papers that had been scattered about the room.

Still holding his head, Carson Drew said, "I have no idea."

All of a sudden, Nancy's eyes lit up.

"I think I do! Excuse me for a moment." Nancy raced upstairs to her room. Just as she had suspected, her own desk had been rummaged through, and the outline to Mrs. Crown's book was gone!

"What did you find?" Bess asked anxiously when Nancy returned.

"Someone connected to the Crown case is getting very nervous," Nancy said. "They took the outline to Mrs. Crown's book. They may have been looking for the anonymous note, too, but, luckily, that's still in my purse."

"I'll just be relieved when this whole case is solved," Hannah said to everyone. She marched over to the phone. "Mr. Drew, I'm calling the doctor. That blow on the head could have given you a concussion. I'll feel much better after you've been checked over."

Carson Drew managed a faint chuckle. "Okay, Hannah. I'm in no condition to give you any argument."

After Hannah made the call she started to straighten up the den.

"I'll do that, Hannah," Nancy said. "Maybe you could fix Dad a cup of tea."

"Good idea," Hannah agreed. "I'll get dinner started, too."

Dr. Black had wasted no time in responding to Hannah's call. After carefully examining Mr. Drew, he said, "Carson, you've received a nasty blow. I want you to keep an ice pack against the injury for at least an hour. If you feel nauseous or dizzy, notify me at once. Otherwise, a good night's sleep will be the best medicine I can recommend."

Nancy walked the doctor to the front door. "Thank you for coming, Dr. Black," she said. "You're sure Dad's going to be okay?" she added anxiously.

"Actually," Dr. Black replied solemnly, "I'm more concerned right now for your welfare than Carson's."

Nancy blinked in surprise. "Why are you concerned about me?"

"News gets around," the doctor replied. "I heard through the grapevine yesterday that you visited Karen Crown and that you've been asking questions about the Roget robbery."

"I was hired by Mrs. Crown a few hours before her accident," Nancy explained. "Even though Mrs. Crown may be dead, I still want to do everything I can for Karen. I'm convinced that she's innocent."

Dr. Black clearly agreed with Nancy's last statement. "I've been the Crowns' family physician since they moved to River Heights. Karen isn't capable of committing any kind of criminal act." Before leaving the doctor said, "I didn't want to say anything in front of your father, Nancy, but I'd like to caution you to be careful. Monica Crown told me last week that she was checking back into the Roget robbery. Now she's missing."

"Dr. Black, are you saying that you believe Mrs. Crown's accident was something more than just an accident?"

"Frankly, yes," the doctor replied without hesitation. "My guess is that Monica Crown got too close to the person who was responsible for the robbery and for framing Karen."

"I'm starting to form a theory about the accident, too," Nancy said thoughtfully. "Thank you again, Dr. Black, and don't worry. I promise you, I'll be very careful."

Carson Drew went upstairs to bed right after dinner. Nancy, Bess, and George gathered together in the living room. For the next two hours they discussed and rediscussed all the people involved in the case.

"You still haven't talked to Karen Crown's fiancé," Bess reminded Nancy.

"I know," Nancy replied. "Karen said she'd ask Larry to get in touch with me. If I don't hear from him soon, I'll have to track him down. In the meantime, there are several other things I plan to do tomorrow."

"Tomorrow?" George repeated. "I thought we had a tennis date at the club tomorrow."

"We do," Nancy said, "but we're not scheduled to play until ten o'clock. I was hoping you'd let me pick you up early in the morning. I'd like to go to the bottom of the Stone Canyon and have a good look around the area where Mrs. Crown's car crashed." She smiled at George. "And two pairs of eyes are better than one."

"Sure," George readily agreed. "Only what do you think you'll find?"

Nancy replied slowly. "I don't know, but I have a hunch."

"Oh, no." Bess giggled. "I'm almost glad I'm working tomorrow. Being around Nancy when she's checking out one of her hunches tends to make me a little nervous."

George flashed a teasing smile at her cousin. "Bess, your own shadow in broad daylight tends to make you a little nervous."

By eight-thirty the following morning, Nancy and George were at the bottom of Stone Canyon, searching the general area where they had last seen Mrs. Crown's car the night of the accident. The demolished sportscar still had not been towed away. The girls spent forty-five minutes poking around in the deserted ravine. Nancy couldn't hide her disappointment when she said, "Let's call it quits, George."

As they climbed back up the steep cliffside George stopped to catch her breath. "Exactly what did you think we might find down there?"

"I hoped we'd find some kind of clue that would prove that Mrs. Crown is still alive."

"Nancy, why don't you just face it. Mrs. Crown is dead."

"Where's her body then?" Nancy challenged. "It didn't just vanish into thin air!" She gave a sigh and followed George up the steep cliff.

Shortly before noon, Nancy and George were playing tennis on court three at the River Heights Country Club. The two competitive, longtime tennis opponents were engaged in the final points of the second set. George expertly returned Nancy's powerful serve down the line. Nancy raced for the ball and with a two-handed backhand sent it flying over the net. Unfortunately for Nancy, her opponent was already at the net. George volleyed the ball deep into Nancy's court, out of her reach.

"Nice shot, George!" called Nancy. "That's the match." The girls picked up their tennis gear and walked slowly across the well-tended grounds toward the clubhouse.

Nancy nodded toward a party of four men that were just coming off the golf course. "Isn't that Frederick Reese?"

"Yes," George replied, "he's a member of the club. He plays here all the time."

"You didn't say anything about that yesterday when we talked to him at Roget's."

George shrugged. "I've seen him here plenty

of times, but yesterday in his office was the first time I had ever met him."

"I want to shower and change in a hurry," Nancy said, taking longer strides.

"What's the rush?"

"I'd like to go into the lounge and order something to drink. Maybe we can sort of accidentally run into Mr. Reese."

"But we just talked to him yesterday," George said. "Why do you want to see him again?"

"I'm not exactly sure," Nancy admitted, "but I'd like to get a look at his face when I tell him that I know he's having financial problems. Also, I want to see his reaction when I tell him about the break-in at my house last night."

George, who worked part-time at the country club giving tennis lessons, didn't accompany Nancy to the locker room. She told Nancy she'd find a table in the lounge as close to Mr. Reese as possible.

After Nancy had showered and changed, she hurried to the lounge.

George waved and Nancy walked to George's table. As she sat down, George spoke to her and to the two men at the next table. "You'll never guess who I ran into, Nancy."

Nancy smiled at Frederick Reese. Her eyes suddenly caught sight of his companion. It was none other than Tom Owens.

"Mr. Reese, Tom," she said in surprise. "It's nice to see you again."

Frederick Reese gave Nancy a cool nod. Tom Owens, on the other hand, was warm and friendly. "How's everything proceeding on the case? Any developments since we spoke yesterday?"

Nancy watched both men carefully as she replied, "Yes, I must be getting close to someone, or something. My house was broken into late yesterday afternoon."

Tom Owens's dark brows raised. His handsome face reflected immediate concern. "Was anything taken?"

Frederick Reese's face seemed empty of all expression when Nancy said, "Yes, the outline to the mystery novel Mrs. Crown was working on just before her disappearance."

"I wish the police would give me some definite word about Monica's accident." Frederick Reese sighed. "Why can't they find her body? No one could just walk away from a crash like that one." He stared blankly at the drink he held between his hands. Finally he said, "It's better to know that someone you care about is dead, than not to know what's happened to her."

Tom Owens said, "Come on, Frederick, you two never got along. You always called those mystery novels she wrote 'garbage.'"

Nancy and George exchanged a meaningful glance.

Frederick Reese shot a piercing, angry look at Tom Owens. "I don't think now is the right time to remind me of how poorly Monica and I got along." A moment of awkward silence passed

58

before Mr. Reese abruptly changed the subject. "I hope your father wasn't hurt too badly last night."

Nancy's eyebrows arched in surprise. "How did you know that he was hurt?" she asked quickly.

"I . . . well, that is . . ." Mr. Reese stammered. "I called your father's office this morning. I understood that Monica recently placed all of her legal affairs into the hands of your father's firm. His secretary told me he wasn't coming in until this afternoon. She explained that a burglar had attacked your father."

Nancy wanted to know exactly why Mr. Reese had called her father, but all she said was, "Dad's fine, thank you. He still has a slight headache, but that's all."

Nancy pulled out her notebook. "Mr. Reese, do you happen to know the address of Mrs. Crown's secretary?"

"You mean Madeline Simmons?" Tom Owens asked.

"Yes, do you know her?" Nancy asked.

Tom smiled and nodded. "Yes, Madeline and I use to date each other quite a lot. She's a lovely lady. Would you like her phone number, too?"

Nancy jotted down the information Tom Owens gave her. She and George were getting ready to leave when a waiter carrying a cordless telephone receiver walked up to Mr. Reese. "Excuse me, sir. You have an important phone call from the River Heights Police Department."

Nancy, George, and Tom Owens watched as Mr. Reese cleared his throat and said nervously into the receiver, "This is Frederick Reese speaking." He listened for a few seconds. Then his face went white. He whispered, "Oh, no!" He nodded once or twice before he wordlessly clicked off the dial tone and placed the receiver on the table.

He said, his voice choked with emotion, "About half a mile from where Monica crashed, the police found a torn piece of black velvet. Monica's housekeeper has identified the material. It's part of the outfit my sister was wearing the night of the accident!"

6

A Clue in Black Velvet

"My sister is really dead!" Frederick Reese seemed close to tears. "Until now"—he choked back a sob—"I thought there might have been a chance she wasn't in that wrecked car."

Tom Owens placed a comforting hand on Mr. Reese's arm. He said, "Fred, you had to face it sooner or later. Monica is gone."

Nancy said kindly, "Mr. Reese, I'm very sorry." Frederick Reese accepted Nancy's condolences with a silent nod of his head.

Nancy and George excused themselves and headed for the parking lot. When they were outside Nancy said, "This latest information makes me feel sure that Mrs. Crown is still alive!"

George stopped dead in her tracks. Disbelief was clearly written all over her face. "Nancy, what are you talking about? If the police found a piece of her clothing near the wreck, that only proves she was in the car. Even Mr. Reese is convinced now that his sister is dead."

"I've had a hunch all along that she's still alive," Nancy said as she got into her car. She seemed so positive that George dropped her argument and listened carefully as Nancy continued. "I think Mrs. Crown deliberately tore her clothing and placed the piece of black velvet where it could be easily found. Now whoever was threatening her will believe she is dead."

Nancy started to back her car out of the parking space. She called out to George, "See you tomorrow night."

Ned was coming home for the weekend. They had planned to spend all day Saturday at the Nickerson mountain cabin. Later that evening they were meeting Bess and George for dinner back in River Heights.

Before going to meet Mrs. Crown's secretary, Nancy stopped by her house. She found her father at his desk, shuffling through some important-looking papers.

"Dad!" Nancy exclaimed. "You should be resting, not working!"

"I feel much better. And I'm glad you're back," Mr. Drew said. "Bess just called. She wants you to stop by Norman's Photography Studio. Bess seems to think she has some information about the Crown case."

Nancy was immediately curious. "Really? I wonder what it could be?"

"I don't know. She just asked me to make sure you got the message."

"Thanks, Dad, I'll stop there on my way over to Montclair."

"Who are you seeing in Montclair?"

"Mrs. Crown's secretary, Madeline Simmons, lives there. Tom Owens just gave me directions to her place."

"You saw Tom Owens again today?"

Nancy nodded. "George and I ran into Tom and Mr. Reese at the country club." Nancy sat on the arm of her father's chair. "Dad, do you know if Mr. Reese might have talked to your secretary today? He knew all about the burglary."

"It's funny that you should ask about Reese," Mr. Drew replied holding up one of the papers he had been studying. "I was just going through some of Monica Crown's legal papers. I found this IOU signed by her brother."

"How much does he owe Mrs. Crown?"

"One hundred thousand dollars," Mr. Drew replied.

Nancy whistled softly. "I guess Tom Owens knew what he was talking about when he told George and me that Frederick Reese was in financial trouble."

Mr. Drew held up his hand. "Wait, there's more. My secretary phoned right after she spoke to Reese earlier this morning. He was inquiring about a second loan. He said his sister was working on the loan papers with her bankers just days before the accident."

63

"Mr. Reese must be in desperate need of money," Nancy said. "Tom said he had made some bad investments."

After Nancy left her father, she headed straight for Norman's Photography Studio, located in a small mall at the edge of town. The studio was owned by family friends of the Marvins, and Bess was temporarily working there while one of the regular employees was on vacation.

A faint jingle of bells signaled Nancy's presence in the shop. Bess immediately left her position behind the counter and hurried to greet Nancy. She whispered, "I'm glad you got my message. Follow me." To a coworker she said, "Don, could you handle things alone here for a few minutes? I'll be right back."

Nancy followed Bess to one of the small rooms in the rear of the studio. "Why all the secrecy?" Nancy suddenly realized that she was whispering, too. "What's this all about anyway?" she asked in a normal tone of voice.

Bess smiled mysteriously. "Remember Tony Adams?" she asked.

Nancy nodded. "He was at the scene of the accident Tuesday night. It's not easy to forget someone with such charming manners," Nancy added sarcastically.

"Well, he was in here this morning. He came to pick up some photos he'd had developed. When he started to pay for them, he discovered he didn't have enough money. He said he'd be back tomorrow. After he left, I took a peek at the pictures."

Bess opened the envelope and spread thirty-six snapshots onto the tabletop. "Most of them are from some rock concert he performed in, but look at these."

Nancy bent closer to get a good look at the three snapshots Bess had separated from the others. One was a picture of Tony and Paul Reese together. They were both clowning around with guitars, but the most interesting part of the picture was Monica Crown's sportscar in the background. A second picture, taken in front of Roget's, was of Paul and his father. The third showed the front of Mrs. Crown's car on a jack two feet off the ground. On his back, next to the car, was Tony Adams. He had a wrench in one hand.

Nancy carefully inspected every detail in the last picture. When she looked up she said, "I suppose Paul and Tony could have become friends. After all, Tony's mother has worked for Mrs. Crown for twenty years. He's lived on the Crown estate practically his entire life."

"And Paul could have met him when he visited his aunt," Bess said.

"Probably," Nancy agreed, "even though there doesn't seem to be any love lost between the Reeses and Mrs. Crown."

"This is the picture I really wanted you to see." Bess pointed to Tony under the sportscar.

"If Tony did tamper with Mrs. Crown's car, that would blow my theory," Nancy said.

She quickly told Bess her theory that Mrs. Crown was still alive. After a thoughtful pause Nancy said, "No, I still think Mrs. Crown has faked her own death."

The girls returned to the front of the studio. "Thanks, Bess," Nancy said. "I'm not sure if the pictures are important to the case or not, but I'm glad you showed them to me." She said goodbye and left the shop.

Nancy had called ahead to set up an appointment with Madeline Simmons. Tom Owens's directions were easy to follow, and the drive to Montclair didn't take long. A few minutes before two o'clock, Nancy was headed up the steps of a luxury apartment building.

Her light rap on the door was answered at once. Madeline Simmons appeared friendly but highly nervous. She shook hands with Nancy and invited her inside. After Nancy was seated, Madeline's first words were, "You weren't followed here, were you?"

"No . . . at least I don't think so," Nancy replied in a startled voice.

Madeline gave a sigh of relief. "Mrs. Crown told me she was planning to ask for your assistance," she said. "Have you found out anything at all about her disappearance?"

Nancy shook her head slowly. "Nothing definite. That's why I'm here. I was hoping you might be able to help me."

Madeline looked surprised. "Believe me, I'm as baffled by Mrs. Crown's disappearance as everyone else. Just because I'm her secretary everyone seems to think . . ." Madeline's words trailed off and she looked down at the floor.

Nancy guessed that Madeline Simmons was about thirty. With silky dark hair, velvety brown eyes, and an almost perfect figure, she could see why Tom Owens had been attracted to the pretty secretary. "I understand you used to date Tom Owens."

Madeline looked up and said in an annoyed voice, "I don't want to discuss him. Not now—or ever."

"I'm sorry," Nancy apologized. "I didn't mean to pry into your personal life." To change the subject, she motioned toward several large packing boxes in the corner of the living room. "Are you planning to move?"

"After all those threatening phone calls I've been getting, I have no choice," replied Madeline. She shuddered. "That awful, weird voice . . ."

Nancy suddenly remembered that Mrs. Crown had mentioned some sort of electronic device when she had described her threatening calls.

Nancy leaned forward in her chair. "What did the caller say to you?"

Madeline swallowed and fought to steady her

67

voice. "Each time that frightening voice ordered me to get a copy of Mrs. Crown's latest manuscript. I told the voice over and over that I didn't have a copy and that I'd never even seen a copy." Madeline looked at Nancy, her eyes wide with fear. "The caller told me to deliver the manuscript to a post office box number. And if I didn't . . ."

"If you didn't . . . ?" Nancy prompted.

Madeline took a breath and forced out her next words: "The police would find my body at the bottom of Stone Canyon."

Nancy said soothingly, "Well, I don't think you'll be getting any more calls now." She told Madeline Simmons about the stolen manuscript and outline.

Madeline shook her head several times. "I don't care. I'm leaving."

Nancy sat up and paced around the small living room. She glanced out the front window. She drew in a sharp, startled breath. A white sedan was parked across the street! Nancy decided not to say anything about it to Madeline Simmons. The young woman was already frightened enough.

Both Nancy and Madeline gave an involuntary jump at the first shrill ring of the telephone.

Madeline stared at the telephone on the table next to her. It rang a second time. With eyes filled with fear, she looked up helplessly at Nancy. "It'll be that voice again," she cried in panic. "I just know it."

68

In the middle of the third ring, Nancy lifted the receiver to her ear.

An electronic robotlike voice gave a command. "Let me speak to Nancy Drew."

Nancy's heart was pounding, but her voice remained calm. "This is Nancy Drew speaking."

"Miss Teenage Detective, you've meddled in other people's business long enough." The bizarre coldness of the electronic voice sent chills up Nancy's spine. "If you value your life, give up the Crown case *now!*"

7

Explosive Experience

Nancy's hand shook as she hung up the receiver. She was surprised to find the call had unnerved her. She took a deep breath and said in a steady voice, "I understand now why you didn't want to take that call, Ms. Simmons. Listening to a robot make threats on your life can be pretty scary."

Madeline was more upset than ever. She folded her arms tight against her to control her trembling body. "What did he . . . *it* have to say this time?"

"The call was for me," Nancy said. "I was warned to stop my investigation of the Crown case."

"But . . . I don't understand . . . how did he know he'd find you here?"

"I'm sorry, Ms. Simmons," Nancy apologized, "but I guess I *was* followed here. A white sedan

70

tailed me several days ago. While we were talking earlier, I glanced out the window and saw it parked across the street." As she spoke, Nancy moved toward the window. "It's gone now. Whoever it was, he or she evidently has a car phone."

Madeline glanced at her watch. "Ms. Drew, you're going to have to excuse me. My flight to Chicago leaves in an hour, and any minute now I have a taxi coming to drive me to the airport." She ushered Nancy to the door.

So much for Madeline Simmons, Nancy thought as she drove home. She was glad she was going up to Cedar Lake the next day. She definitely deserved a day off!

The next morning, during the drive from River Heights to the Nickerson cabin at Cedar Lake, Nancy told Ned what had happened so far in the Crown case. After she recounted her meeting with Madeline Simmons, Ned asked, "Do you think the phone call came from whoever was in the white car?"

Nancy replied, "I'm not sure, but whoever is behind the wheel of that car has been keeping close tabs on me for the past few days."

Ned carefully guided the car around the narrow curved road that led to the lake. "How serious do you think this 'robot caller' is, Nancy? Do you think he might try to carry out his threats?"

"Well, it's pretty obvious that the person who

71

started out as a diamond thief is getting desperate now," Nancy said. "He or she might do anything to keep from getting caught." Nancy looked grim when she added, "I'll just have to be super cautious from now on."

Ned reached over and took Nancy's hand. She felt a gentle squeeze of his fingers around hers. Her serious expression disappeared and was replaced with a happy smile.

When they reached the Nickersons' rustic but comfortable weekend cabin, Ned's parents stepped outside to greet them. They chatted together for a little while, then Ned asked his father, "Dad, do you mind if I take the boat out? I want to give Nancy a spin around the lake."

"Sure, Ned," Mr. Nickerson said with a smile for both his son and Nancy. "You two have a good time."

During the summer months, Ned and Nancy often water-skied over the flat, smooth surface of the lake. But now, in mid-October, the lake had turned cold and choppy. Before getting into the boat, Nancy bundled up in a down jacket.

The lake wasn't crowded at this time of year. Nancy had noticed only half a dozen boats during the first hour of the leisurely cruise about Cedar Lake's familiar coves and inlets.

"This is terrific, Ned," Nancy said happily. "The lake is great this time of year."

"Yeah, it is," Ned replied. "I'm glad you could make it today, because I might not be able to get away from school for the next few weeks. I've got some big exams coming up."

Ned slowed the boat so that it idled lazily in a quiet cove. The area around the shore was wooded, and in this secluded spot Nancy felt as if she and Ned were alone in the world.

Their privacy was suddenly shattered by the deafening roar of a speeding boat. Ned shifted gears and maneuvered their small boat out of the cove and into the open lake. Both Nancy and Ned spotted the other boat instantly. Loud shouts and wild laughter could be heard above the sound of its motor. The speeding boat was aimed like a bullet straight toward a small rowboat anchored near the far shore. At the last possible second, it veered sharply to the right, just missing the rowboat and its single occupant, an elderly fisherman.

"Nancy," Ned shouted as he headed the boat across the lake, "there's a pair of binoculars in the chest behind the seat. See if you can get the name on that boat."

Nancy fought hard to keep her balance and managed to open the chest. She grabbed the binoculars and returned to her seat. She quickly focused in on the recklessly speeding boat. It was now zooming straight toward another small, helpless rowboat. "Well, its name is appropriate anyway," Nancy said dryly. "It's *Paul's Cyclone.*" Nancy gasped suddenly. "Ned, you won't believe who's in that boat! Paul Reese and Tony Adams!"

"I'm going to see if we can head them off before they hurt someone!" Ned shouted, stepping on the gas. By the time Ned and Nancy had reached the center of the lake, *Paul's Cyclone* had managed a second near-collision.

When he spotted Ned's boat, Paul Reese gave a shout of defiance. He turned his speeding boat toward Nancy and Ned.

"Oh, no," Nancy whispered under her breath when she realized that *Paul's Cyclone* was headed straight for them!

Ned's fingers tightened on the steering wheel. "Hold on, Nancy!" He swerved to the right, narrowly avoiding a collision. But the sharp turn, combined with the raging wake crested by *Paul's Cyclone* almost capsized them. As they were rocked violently back and forth, Paul Reese recklessly circled around them at high speed. When Paul recognized the occupants of the boat he was aiming for, he yelled, "Hey, Tony! It's the teen-age detective and her hotshot boyfriend."

Tony stood up and cried, "Ahoy!" at the top of his lungs. Then he fell back into his seat and doubled over with laughter.

Paul stopped laughing long enough for a final jeering shout, "Is the Monica Crown case scaring you, Ms. Detective? Well, you're not going to find too many clues out here!" With these words Paul pushed the throttle wide open. *Paul's Cyclone* tore off across the lake, around a bend, and out of sight.

"What a pair," Ned said shaking his head.

"A pair of jerks!" Nancy declared angrily.

Later that evening, Nancy and Ned met George and Bess at Pasta Pizzazz, an Italian restaurant in River Heights. The four friends had a good time talking, laughing, and eating.

"Oh, no . . ." Ned suddenly groaned. "Look who's here." Everyone at the table followed his gaze.

Paul Reese and Tony Adams had just entered the restaurant.

"Those two are real trouble," Nancy said. "Ned and I had a run-in with them today." She told Bess and George about the incident at the lake.

Paul was about to take a seat when he caught sight of Nancy and Ned. He tapped Tony on the shoulder and pointed. The two young men made their way through the crowd of diners toward Nancy's table.

"Well, what do you know?" Tony Adams said in a loud voice. "We seem to run into Mr. Athlete and Ms. Detective wherever we go."

Paul's eyes narrowed. "Yeah, just our bad luck, I guess." He looked accusingly at Nancy. "You reported us to the lake patrol, didn't you?"

Ned leaned forward in his chair. "She didn't, I did. You could have hurt a lot of people out there today."

Tony glared at Ned. "You don't look like you've

changed much, Nickerson. I suppose you're a big man on the college campus, just the way you were in high school."

Nancy could see that Ned was fighting to control his temper. In an even voice he said, "You haven't changed either, Adams. I'd say you're still the same punk you always were."

Tony took an angry step forward. Paul placed a warning hand on his arm. "Forget it, Tony. Let's go." Without another word Paul and Tony walked back to their own table.

"Tony Adams went to River Heights High?" asked Nancy.

Ned nodded. "Yes, he was suspended in his junior year for stealing a car. It turned out that he was a part of a gang that hot-wired cars and stripped them for their parts. He spent several months in a juvenile prison."

Bess shuddered. "They both give me the creeps. It's nearly midnight. Maybe we should be heading home."

In the parking lot outside Pasta Pizzazz, Nancy and Ned said goodbye to Bess and George. On the drive home Nancy again voiced her thoughts about Mrs. Crown's disappearance. "If there was only some way I could get hold of the manuscript she was working on. I'm sure it would shed some light on this mystery."

"You know what?" Ned asked.

"What?"

"There's never a dull moment when you're

around." In the soft glow from the lighted panel, Ned's eyes met Nancy's.

When they got to Nancy's house, Ned walked Nancy up the steps to the front door. They both noticed an envelope taped to the mailbox.

Nancy felt her pulse quicken. She had no doubt that the envelope had something to do with the case. Ned leaned over and yanked the envelope from the mailbox. Without warning there was a sudden, blinding explosion!

8

A Desperate Message

The explosion awakened Carson Drew from a sound sleep. His first thought was of Nancy. He darted down the stairs and threw open the front door. Nancy and Ned were enveloped in a cloud of smoke. As the smoke started to thin out, Mr. Drew could see that they were unharmed. He wrapped his arms around his daughter. "Nancy, Ned, are you all right? What happened?"

It was several minutes before either Nancy or Ned could speak. They went inside the house, coughing and gasping for air. Their eyes were burning from the gases let off in the explosion. Tears streamed down their faces.

Hannah Gruen had heard the explosion in her room, too. She was wrapping a bathrobe around herself when she caught sight of Nancy and Ned still trying to catch their breaths.

She rushed over to them and cried, "Are you all right?"

Nancy nodded and gave the housekeeper a reassuring hug. "Yes . . . we're okay."

"Hannah," Ned said wiping his eyes with the back of his hands, "could you get us a couple of washcloths?"

Nancy and Ned were seated side by side on the couch when Hannah returned. They placed the wet cloths over their eyes. After several minutes, the burning sensations in their eyes subsided.

"I think I'll fix us all a cup of tea," Hannah said once she was sure the two young people were going to be all right.

Carson Drew returned from checking the mailbox and announced, "When you pulled the envelope off, you also pulled an attached string that was rigged to a loud but not very dangerous explosive."

"So it was just one more warning from the Roget's thief," Nancy said wearily.

"It looks that way," her father answered. "I'll call the police right now. They'll probably dust the box for fingerprints tomorrow, but I'm sure whoever planted the device was smart enough not to leave prints behind."

Everyone had calmed down by the time they had finished the tea and cookies Hannah served. When Nancy walked Ned to the front door she forced a tired smile and said softly, "As you said earlier—never a dull moment."

Nancy stayed close to home on Sunday. Early that morning, the police had come to the house to check out the mailbox. After they had gone, Nancy's father left to catch a flight to New York so that he could be well rested and prepared for a Monday morning business conference in that city. Ned had returned to Emerson, and Bess and George were at a family reunion in nearby Montclair.

Nancy was happy to have some time by herself. She spent the day quietly. After she read the Sunday paper, she curled up in a chair by the fireplace with a book.

The phone rang shortly after two o'clock. Nancy took the call at her father's large mahogany desk in the den. She automatically reached for a pen as she lifted the receiver.

The voice on the other end said, "Hello, my name is Larry Holtz. I'd like to speak to Nancy Drew."

"This is Nancy Drew speaking." Nancy felt a rush of excitement. For days she had waited to talk to Karen Crown's fiancé.

Larry Holtz said, "I've just come from seeing Karen. She seems to think you're going to get her out of that rotten place."

"I'm working on it, Mr. Holtz," replied Nancy.

"What exactly does that mean? You're 'working on it'?" Larry Holtz made no effort to hide his irritation. "I resent you coming up here and giving Karen false hope."

"Mr. Holtz," Nancy remained cool and confident. "I'd like you to know I don't feel I was giving Karen false hope. I believe in her innocence and—"

"So what?" Larry interrupted. Nancy could hear the bitterness behind his words. "I believe in her innocence, too. What good is that going to do?"

"Please believe me, I'm doing everything I can to find the real thief. I'm sure I'm on the right track. It's just a matter of time, and—"

Again Nancy was interrupted. "Time! Karen has already been in that terrible place for months!" Larry's voice choked with emotion. When he spoke again his voice was steady, but he sounded exhausted and without hope. "I'm . . . sorry, Ms. Drew. I shouldn't take this out on you. It's only that I'm not sure how much more Karen can take. I'm worried that she'll have a breakdown if she has to stay in prison much longer."

"I understand, Mr. Holtz," Nancy said sympathetically. "I know how hard it is for Karen and you right now. But I'm sure I'm close to breaking the case. Someone has been following me, and I've received several threats in the past few days. I think that's a sign that the real thief is getting very nervous."

Larry sounded slightly more hopeful. "I only hope you're right, Ms. Drew." There was a long silence on the line before he continued. "I'm going to be in River Heights tomorrow. I have some business at Roget's. Perhaps we could get together. I'm not sure that I have any helpful information, but I'd feel better if we could talk."

"I'd like to discuss the case with you, too," Nancy said eagerly.

"I'll be coming in on my company's private plane. Could we meet at the airport café for lunch . . . say, about noon tomorrow?"

Then Larry Holtz gave Nancy a description of what he'd be wearing so that she would be able to recognize him.

"I'll be there at noon," Nancy promised.

It was late in the afternoon when Carson Drew called. "Nancy, I'm calling because there seemed to be some confusion about my hotel reservation. I'm now staying at the Carlton. I wanted you to have the number."

"Thanks, Dad." As Nancy jotted down the number, she told her father about the call from Larry Holtz. She was about to hang up when a sudden thought occurred to her. "Dad, if you have any extra time, do you think you could see Mrs. Crown's publishers?"

"Sure, I can arrange to do that," her father readily agreed.

"See if you can get hold of Mrs. Crown's latest manuscript or anything she might have written about the Roget's robbery."

By five-thirty Nancy had finished the book she'd started earlier that day. She was beginning to believe that too much peace and quiet all in one day wasn't necessarily a good thing. She was starting to feel restless instead of rested. Her mood was broken by the persistent ringing of the doorbell. When Nancy opened the door she was astonished to see Allison Phillips. Standing just behind the TV reporter was a cameraman with his Channel 10 minicam pointed straight at Nancy!

Allison Phillips had a big, phony smile on her face as she said, "Hi, Ms. Drew. I'm sure you remember me. We met earlier this week at the site of Monica Crown's unfortunate accident."

"Yes, I—"

Allison, speaking into a hand microphone, deliberately interrupted Nancy's reply. She continued with her well-practiced TV chatter, and at the same time she managed to push her way past Nancy into the house.

"Ms. Phillips, I think I told you I didn't want to be interviewed, and I—" Nancy began.

"Call me Allison," the reporter said with a sweet but condescending smile. "Let me explain something," she continued. "As the Channel Ten field reporter I've been doing a week-long series on local crime."

"I don't understand what that has to do with—" Once again Nancy's words were cut off.

"I just came from the police department. I understand that last Thursday someone broke into your home and attacked your father. I also understand that just last night you were the victim of—"

Nancy didn't lose her temper very often, but when she did it was usually for a good reason. This time it was Nancy who interrupted Allison. "Allison, before you go on with this, I have something I'd like to say." Nancy was polite, but there was an unmistakable tone in her voice that, temporarily at least, silenced Allison Phillips. "You cannot interview someone in the privacy of her home without being invited to do so." Nancy's blue eyes darkened a shade, and her cheeks flushed slightly. "I have no intention of being a part of your local crime spot on tonight's news broadcast."

Nancy continued, still without raising her voice, "You and your cameraman had better leave my house right now."

"Jason, wait for me outside. No—go to the van and call the station. Tell them we'll be back within the hour. Tell them we'll go on the air tonight with the footage we shot at the police station."

All the while Allison was ordering the cameraman about, her smile never faded. It occurred to Nancy that the smile seemed to be the TV reporter's one and only expression.

Just as the cameraman left, Hannah came in from the kitchen. "Oh, do we have a guest?" she asked pleasantly.

"No," Nancy stated emphatically.

"Oh . . ." Hannah suddenly became aware of

the tension between the two young women. "Well," she said awkwardly, "excuse me. I . . . I'd better check on a cake I have in the oven."

"Nancy, before I leave, please let me ask just one question," begged Allison Phillips.

Against her better judgment, Nancy relented. "Okay, if you'll give me your word that anything I say will be off the record. I don't want anything I say repeated on your news program."

"Absolutely," Allison agreed. "This is off the record. What I'd like to know is if the break-in on Thursday night and the incident that occurred last night with the explosive were in any way related to the fact that you're trying to prove that Karen Crown was framed for the Roget robbery."

Nancy was surprised that Allison knew so much about her private investigation. She wanted to ask Allison where she'd gotten her information, but she decided that might not be wise. Instead she answered Allison honestly. "Yes, I believe the two incidents are related to the Crown case."

"But how can you possibly hope to prove Karen innocent when some of the Roget diamonds were found in her possession?" The question was asked with the same sweet smile, but there was something about the TV reporter that Nancy didn't trust.

Nancy returned Allison's smile. "We agreed on just one question, remember?" With those words, Nancy reached behind Allison and pulled open the front door.

Nancy had just finished dinner when the phone rang. The voice on the other end of the line was confused, and nearly hysterical. "Miss Drew, I'm Al Morris's wife. I . . . he . . . that is . . ."

"You're the wife of the security guard at Roget's?"

The woman replied shakily, "Yes, we . . . Al . . . Al is being admitted to the community hospital. Miss Drew . . . he insists on speaking to you. He says it's urgent. I think he wants to tell you something about the night of the robbery!"

Twenty minutes later Nancy was dashing across the hospital parking lot to the emergency room.

The room was packed with doctors, orderlies, nurses, attendants, and patients and their families. Suddenly, a frail gray-haired woman approached her. "You must be Nancy Drew. Al said you had long blond hair and that you were very young.

"Al has had a heart attack. He's over here." Mrs. Morris led Nancy to a bed on the far side of the emergency room. A nurse was bending over the stricken security guard. She seemed to be adjusting some of the life-saving equipment connected to him.

The nurse gave Nancy a businesslike smile. "I'm glad you're here. He's been asking for you. If he can get whatever it is that's bothering him off his mind, it might help calm him down." She added firmly, "But please make it short. We don't want him to become agitated."

Nancy leaned over the bed's raised guard railing. She spoke quietly and directly into Al Morris's ear. "Mr. Morris, it's Nancy Drew. I'm here."

The security guard's eyes blinked. "Nan . . . Nancy?"

"Yes. Mr. Morris, what is it you wanted to tell me?"

Al Morris lifted his right hand. Nancy took the man's hand in her own. With all of his remaining strength, Al whispered, "Karen . . . Crown . . . she . . . she's innocent. I want to clear my conscience . . . want you to know who . . . who really did it." Suddenly Nancy felt Al Morris's grip on her hand loosen. His eyes fluttered and then closed!

9

Larry Holtz

The nurse pushed Nancy aside and yelled, "Code One!" Immediately Al Morris was surrounded by a well-trained medical staff. A doctor called over his shoulder, "Mrs. Morris, we're taking your husband away to run some tests. We've managed to stabilize his vital signs, but it might be hours, even days, before he regains consciousness. He's slipped into a coma."

The doctor looked at Nancy. "Perhaps you can drive Mrs. Morris home."

"Of course," Nancy replied.

The Morris home was located in a run-down section of River Heights. The inside of their house was well kept and clean, but clearly there was little money for extra comforts.

"Thank you for the ride home, Nancy." Mrs. Morris removed her overcoat and laid it over the back of a worn chair. "With Al in the hospital I just don't . . ." Mrs. Morris began to cry softly.

"Mrs. Morris," Nancy said, "is there anything I can do for you before I leave?"

"No, thank you, dear," Mrs. Morris answered. "I hope Al was able to tell you whatever it was that's been bothering him."

"He wanted to tell me about the diamond robbery," Nancy said as kindly as possible. "But he wasn't able to tell me everything before he slipped into the coma."

"It's a funny thing about that robbery," Mrs. Morris said. "Ever since that time, things have been much easier for Al and me. Even though Roget's lost a million dollars' worth of diamonds, Mr. Reese was nice enough to give Al a big raise."

Nancy didn't want to upset Mrs. Morris by suggesting that the raise might have been a bribe to persuade Al to drug himself and allow the thief inside Roget's. Nancy was now convinced that this was exactly what had happened. Al Morris had been just seconds away from revealing the real thief's name!

Nancy stayed with Mrs. Morris for almost an hour. She left only when she was sure that the older woman was calm enough to be alone.

Nancy returned home. She was getting ready for bed when the phone rang.

"Hello," Nancy said.

That was the first and last word that an excited Bess allowed Nancy to say during the remainder of their telephone conversation. "Nancy, I'm listening to the Channel Ten news. They've just broken for a commercial. They said that when they return, Allison Phillips will have some inside information about Karen Crown! I'm hanging up now. Hurry, turn on your TV!"

There was a click and then the steady hum of the dial tone. Nancy laughed as she replaced the receiver. She took three quick steps to her bedroom dresser and snapped on a small portable TV. As the picture came into focus, the commercial ended. It was followed by a picture of a pretty, smiling Allison Phillips.

Allison spoke into the camera with an air of importance and authority. "Last Monday night Monica Crown disappeared in an automobile accident in Stone Canyon. Her body has not yet been found. The only evidence that she was in the crash is a piece of black velvet, found near the accident, that came from the outfit Mrs. Crown had been wearing earlier the same night."

Allison continued, "Mrs. Crown's daughter, Karen Crown, was tried and convicted several months ago for the Roget diamond robbery. She is presently serving a three-year prison sentence.

"My crime scoop for this Sunday evening is that I have just come from a private interview with Nancy Drew, the young River Heights detective who was hired by Mrs. Crown shortly before her disappearance. Ms. Drew, in an exclusive interview, told me that she plans to prove

Karen Crown innocent of all wrongdoing. It appears that Nancy Drew is on to something, because she has received two warnings from the person she suspects of being the real criminal. I will keep you posted as this story continues to unfold."

Nancy glared at the television screen until Allison's image was replaced by the Channel 10 anchorman. Nancy angrily snapped off the set. "Allison Phillips," she said, fuming, "if I ever get the chance to see you again, watch out!"

At eleven-thirty the next morning Nancy was about to leave for her lunch date with Larry Holtz. As she slipped on her tan jacket, the front doorbell rang. "I'll get it, Hannah," Nancy called.

When she opened the door, Nancy was surprised to see Ned standing there. "Hi," he said with a grin.

"Hi," she said, clearly delighted to see him. "What are you doing here?"

"I left for Emerson early yesterday," Ned explained, "but I never made it. My car broke down. I spent most of the morning getting it towed to a garage. While it's being repaired, I'm using my mother's car. I'm heading back to campus later this afternoon, but I thought maybe we could have lunch first."

"I'm having lunch with Larry Holtz. You remember—I told you about him. He's Karen

91

Crown's fiancé. I'm supposed to meet him at the airport at noon. Why don't you join us?"

"Okay," Ned agreed. "Let's go." He paused for a moment. "Whose car should we take?"

"Let's take yours," suggested Nancy. "I feel like being a passenger for a change."

During the ten-minute ride to the airport, Nancy happened to glance in the side-view mirror. She saw a white sedan not far behind them. She stiffened. Ned had spotted the car at the same time. He nodded toward the rearview mirror. "I hate to mention it, but your friend in the white car is on your tail again."

Both Nancy and Ned kept a close eye on the car behind them. Before they reached the airport, the car had turned off onto a side road. "Maybe we're both being overly suspicious," Nancy said hopefully. "I mean, there has to be more than one white sedan in this town."

When they got to the airport café, they found Larry Holtz already seated at a table. He stood up as they approached him. "Ms. Drew?"

"Yes," Nancy replied with a friendly smile. "Please call me Nancy. I'd like you to meet a friend of mine, Ned Nickerson."

It didn't take Nancy long to decide that she liked Larry Holtz. She only hoped that Larry was as honest and trustworthy as he was likable. As a detective, Nancy knew she had to suspect everyone involved with Roget's.

Nancy related the events of Sunday night and

her meeting with Al Morris. "Al told me Karen was innocent. I'm sure he was about to tell me the name of the diamond thief before he lapsed into a coma."

Larry asked quickly, "That's all he said?"

A slight frown crossed Nancy's forehead. "Yes, that's all. I'm sorry." She added quickly, "But I'm going to call the hospital later today. I want to see him again as soon as he's better."

"*If* he gets better," Larry said gloomily. "The way Karen's luck has been running, Al Morris will die before he can tell us anything."

Nancy said in an understanding tone, "I know how you feel, Larry, but you'll see, everything is going to work out."

Larry nodded, but he didn't seem too convinced.

Nancy and Ned exchanged a glance. Finally, Nancy said, "Larry, I understand that it was you who brought the six stolen diamonds to Roget's. Did Mr. Reese have a buyer for them?"

"No," Larry said. "Mr. Reese wanted them to be cut by Tom Owens before trying to sell them. Tom is—or was—the best stonecutter in the business. It was at that same time that Tom's arthritis was diagnosed. When Mr. Reese learned about his condition, he forced Tom to quit."

"Couldn't Reese have kept Owens on the job, at least for a while?" Ned asked.

"No, not really. You see, a stonecutter must be able to make very exact, precise movements.

Tom's fingers are already stiff. Eventually his hands will become completely crippled," Larry explained. "No one, not even Tom, can blame Mr. Reese for not keeping him."

"Since you work for a company that buys, sells, and trades precious jewels, isn't it possible that word might leak back to you once the diamonds have been fenced?" Nancy asked.

"The diamonds are still very 'hot,'" Larry told Nancy. "I doubt that the thief wants to take a chance on fencing them just now. He'll probably hold on to them until things quiet down."

Ned gazed admiringly out the window at Larry's private company plane, which was parked near the closest runway. It had the name of Larry's company on it in large silver letters. "That's a great-looking airplane, Larry. How long have you been flying?"

The worried look that Larry had worn throughout most of the lunch disappeared as he started to talk about flying. "I got my pilot's license when I was seventeen. I've flown a lot of small planes since then, but nothing handles as well as this one." He grinned at Nancy and Ned. "Would you two like a ride?"

"We'd definitely like a ride, wouldn't we, Nancy?" Ned's enthusiasm brought a laugh from Larry as well as Nancy.

"Oh, definitely," Nancy agreed.

When Nancy and Ned had seated themselves

in the plane, Larry said, "Oh, I forgot my briefcase. I must have left it in the restaurant. I'll be right back." He ran off. Ten minutes later he returned carrying the briefcase. "Can you believe it?" he said, as he got into the plane. "The waitress thought this was luggage, and she took it to the check-in counter!"

Minutes later Larry's plane roared down the runway and lifted off the ground with ease. As the plane gained altitude, Larry turned toward the foothills west of River Heights. Nancy and Ned enjoyed the aerial view of all the familiar sights below.

"We're flying over Stone Canyon now," Larry told them.

"That's rugged terrain down there," Ned said thoughtfully.

"Yes," Larry said. "I hate to think that Mrs. Crown might have spent days wandering around in that canyon."

"Then you think she's still alive," Nancy said excitedly. "So do I."

"So does Karen, because of the piece of black velvet that was found," Larry said, "but I don't buy it. I'm sure she's dead. Sooner or later her body will turn up."

Larry had just pointed the plane back toward the airport when a cracking sound caused the small aircraft to shudder. The shudder turned into a violent and steady shake.

The plane's pilot and two passengers were

being jolted back and forth in their seats when a second crack sounded with tremendous force and black fluid spattered across the windshield. "It's the oil pump!" Larry shouted. He clutched the wildly vibrating steering wheel tightly in both hands. "Hang on! We're going down!"

10

Terror in the Sky

The next ten minutes were the longest and most frightening of Nancy's life. There was zero visibility out the front windshield, which was now totally covered with oil. Larry cranked his side window open and leaned out as far as he could.

Nancy and Ned found themselves helpless in the situation. The only way they could assist the pilot was not to panic. Nancy glanced over her shoulder and forced a worried smile at Ned who was seated in the rear seat. Ned smiled back and put a comforting hand on Nancy's arm.

The motor started to cough and sputter. Then with a final choke the engine died. The only sound inside the plane was that of the wind whistling through Larry's open window.

Larry pulled his head back inside and yelled, "I've spotted the airport! We're still high enough so that we may be able to glide in." He gave them both an encouraging thumbs-up signal. "Just keep your fingers crossed."

The plane was rapidly losing altitude. They were coming closer to the ground each second. From her side window Nancy realized they had just cleared a set of high wires. Suddenly she saw the blur of trees and the tops of buildings that she recognized as airplane hangars. They had made it to the runway! The plane touched down, bounced in the air, and then touched down a second time with a thud. The sound of the screeching brakes pierced Nancy's eardrums. The wheels had locked. The plane veered dangerously off the runway!

When the plane came to a stop at last, Nancy, Ned, and Larry all breathed a big sigh of relief. They unbuckled their safety belts and scrambled from the plane as quickly as possible.

It took several moments for the three young people to recover from the shock of near death. Nancy and Ned hugged each other. At last Nancy released Ned and turned to Larry. "You did a great job of getting us back here in one piece, Larry. Thanks."

"What happened anyway?" Ned asked.

Larry frowned. "I'm not sure. I'm going to have one of the mechanics check out the plane right now."

A dozen or so people from the airport were racing toward the stricken plane. Several mechanics were among the group. It didn't take long for them to reach an unanimous conclusion. Someone had tampered with the plane. One of the mechanics pointed to the severed oil pump. "That's a new pump. No way would it have torn open on its own. It's been cut by a sharp instrument. And look at this. The fuel pump has been punctured."

Larry inspected the sabotaged fuel pump. "No wonder the engine quit on us. We were out of gas."

"You three are very lucky," the mechanic said. "One of you must have a powerful enemy."

Nancy nodded and replied solemnly, "One of us definitely does. Ned, would you mind taking me home now? I want to report this to the police right away."

Later that afternoon Police Chief McGinnis motioned Nancy toward a chair. He sat back down behind his cluttered desk and smiled at her pleasantly. McGinnis was an old friend of both Nancy and her father. They liked and respected him. For his part, Chief McGinnis admired Nancy's enormous talent for criminal investigation. "I know you're here about Monica Crown's disappearance," the chief said.

Nancy nodded.

"We've stopped searching Stone Canyon, but we're still investigating the case," continued McGinnis. "At this point there's nothing new. If anything does turn up, I'll get in touch with you."

"Thanks, Chief," Nancy said. "I'd appreciate that." Then she changed the subject. "Actually, the main reason I'm here is to tell you about an attempted murder."

"Murder!" exclaimed the chief. He leaned forward and listened attentively as Nancy described the afternoon's near disaster. She also told the chief she thought that she was the intended victim.

"You think someone is out to kill you?" Chief McGinnis asked.

"I think someone just wanted to frighten me off at first. But now I'm not so sure." Nancy described the torn photograph, the phone call she had received at Madeline Simmons's apartment, and she reminded the chief about the explosive device that had been attached to the Drews' mailbox. She also told him about the white sedan that had been trailing her from the beginning of the case.

Chief McGinnis said, "When my men dusted your mailbox for fingerprints they found that the explosive used was relatively harmless. I was pretty sure that someone was playing a prank or just plain trying to scare you." The chief took a while to consider everything that Nancy had told him. Finally he said, "I hope you're taking every precaution, Nancy. It's beginning to sound as if we're dealing with an unbalanced mind."

"I agree," Nancy replied. "It's strange how often insane people can pass themselves off as completely sane."

When Nancy returned home that evening she felt gloomier than she had on any day since she had been on the Crown case. She was tired and shaken from her brush with death on board Larry's plane. Her conversation with Chief McGinnis had left her frustrated. And the almost certain knowledge that whoever had tried to kill her once would try again gave her a cold, tight knot in the pit of her stomach.

Very early Tuesday morning, Nancy called Bess and George and asked them to accompany her on the drive to the State Women's Institution. Nancy still felt frustrated and mildly depressed about how slowly the case seemed to be going. A drive with her two closest friends would help lift her spirits. Nancy also felt the need to speak with Karen Crown one more time.

"The thing that gets me about Allison Phillips," Bess said as they drove along the highway, "is that she had the nerve to go on TV and announce to practically the entire world that you were hot on the trail of the real thief."

"Not to mention the fact that she actually burst into your house last night *uninvited*," George put in.

Nancy kept her eyes on the road as she spoke. "What annoys me the most about Allison is the fact that she broke her word to me. The things I told her about Karen Crown and the Roget diamond robbery were supposed to be off the record."

George leaned forward from her position in the backseat. "The thing that bothers me about Allison Phillips is that fake smile of hers. Have either of you ever noticed that smile?"

"Yes!" Nancy and Bess chorused at the same time. The three girls burst out laughing.

When they arrived at the prison, Bess and George waited in the car while Nancy talked to Karen Crown.

The dark circles under Karen's eyes told Nancy that the young woman hadn't been sleeping well. Karen seated herself across the table from Nancy. She smiled. "I guess it will be a long time before you go flying with my fiancé again, won't it?"

Nancy laughed. "You've talked to Larry?"

Karen's smile deepened. "Yes, he called yesterday about an hour after your near crash."

"I must be getting close to the real diamond thief, Karen. That's why someone tried to have me killed yesterday."

"Are you any closer to finding out what's happened to my mother?" Karen asked. "You know, the more I think about it, the more I'm convinced she's still alive."

"That's why I came today," Nancy said. "I don't want to give you any false hope, but I have a strong hunch, too, that your mother is alive and well. A piece of black velvet from the outfit she was wearing that same night was found on a bush not far from the accident. I think that was your mother's signal to us."

Seeing Karen's happy expression was disturbing to Nancy. She quickly added, "You realize I can't be sure, Karen. As I said, right now it's just a hunch."

"I understand," Karen said. "But it makes me feel much better knowing you're doing everything you can for me, Nancy."

On their way back to River Heights, the three girls stopped for lunch at a quiet country inn not far from the main highway. Both Bess and George had to be back in River Heights by two o'clock. George had a tennis lesson to give at the country club, and Bess had promised to fill in during the late afternoon hours at the photography studio.

"Nancy," Bess said as she stepped out of the car in front of the studio, "my car is in the garage. I'm going to need a ride home. Would you be able to pick me up at five?"

"Sure, I'll be back at five." Nancy waved. "I'll see you then."

Although she had managed to appear relaxed and casual with Bess and George, she had been on constant guard throughout the day. From the moment she had left her house that morning she had been on the lookout for the white sedan or any other suspicious signs that might signal the presence of her unknown enemy.

Nancy had close to three hours before she had to pick up Bess. She headed for the local newspaper offices. After parking her car, she glanced around. Then she hurried into the building. At the information desk, she was given clearance by a clerk to go into the basement archives where microfilm of old newspapers was stored.

The basement was cold and dark. Nancy pulled her jacket closer around her. The diamond robbery had occurred five months before, on May 14. She loaded the May 14 microfilm into a viewing machine and carefully read every word of the article. After she'd finished, Nancy found articles on microfilm from later papers. She searched for any detail that might give her some new insight into the robbery.

Nancy was so deeply absorbed in what she was reading that she didn't hear a creak on the stairs behind her. Then someone whispered in an eerie voice, "Ms. Drew, I see you're still working on the Crown case!"

11

Bess Is Missing

Nancy gasped. She turned in the direction of the voice. In the shadowy darkness of the basement, she was just able to make out the silhouette of a tall man standing at the bottom of the stairs. As he approached her, Nancy saw that it was Paul Reese.

"Paul! You frightened me! Why did you sneak down the stairs like some—" Nancy stopped, realizing that Paul Reese could very well be the person who had been threatening her life. She tensed her body, ready to move quickly if he should attack her.

Paul laughed. He seemed to enjoy Nancy's uncertain expression. "I didn't think anything would scare River Heights' girl detective. Besides, I didn't sneak down here. I saw you enter the building almost forty-five minutes ago. I wanted to talk to you, so I waited outside. I finally got tired of waiting. The desk clerk told me you were down here."

"Well, what do you want?" Nancy was still alarmed, but she managed to give the impression of just being annoyed at Paul's intrusion.

Paul gave Nancy a cocky grin. "Sure sorry to hear about your near plane wreck yesterday."

Nancy raised her eyebrows. "Does that mean you're sorry to hear that it was only a 'near wreck' and not the real thing?"

"No, of course not," Paul replied quickly.

"News travels fast," Nancy said. "How did you find out about the emergency landing?"

"I'm a student at Emerson College, remember? I overheard Ned talking to some of his friends."

"Do you always eavesdrop on other people's conversations?"

Paul ignored Nancy's remark. "Have you found out anything more about my aunt?"

Nancy sighed. "No, I haven't." She changed the subject. "They're having quarter finals at Emerson this week. What are you doing in River Heights, anyway?"

"Not that it's any of your business," Paul said with a careless shrug, "but I needed some quick cash. My dad is a soft touch."

The more Nancy was around Paul, the more she disliked him.

"From what I understand, you're not the only one in your family who's in need of money."

Paul frowned. "What's that supposed to mean?"

"It means that your father is in financial trouble. He needs money a lot more than you do—and he needs a lot more of it."

"You don't know what you're talking about." Paul took a step closer to Nancy. "Why don't you mind your own business!"

Nancy was ready to spring out of her chair if Paul got any closer, but outwardly she remained calm. "When I'm on a case, other people's business *is* my business." Always thinking like a detective, Nancy decided to bait Paul even further. If he was involved in the Roget diamond robbery, maybe she could make him angry enough to reveal some important evidence. She remembered the pictures Bess had shown her at Norman's Photography Studio. "I know that you and Tony Adams tampered with your aunt's car."

Paul gave a snort. "You don't know what you're talking about. Tony works for my aunt. Sometimes he takes care of her car. I just happened to be visiting her one day when he was fixing the engine."

Nancy looked Paul straight in the eyes. "Maybe your aunt discovered that you and Tony knew who the real thief was. You couldn't take the chance that she'd find out who you were covering up for." Nancy turned back to the microfilm machine. "Unless *you're* the thief," she added casually. She knew she was taking a risk by saying all this, but it was a risk she had to take.

"You're nuts!" Paul shouted. He turned and bounded up the basement stairs.

Nancy's hand shook a little as she continued to study the microfilm. From time to time she jotted down names, facts, dates, anything and everything that might later prove to be important. Finally, she removed the last roll of microfilm and snapped off the viewer. She climbed the steps to the main floor. As she was about to leave the building, she spotted Allison Phillips coming in through the revolving door. The young women saw each other at the same time.

Allison spoke first. "I just heard about the close call you had at the airport yesterday."

Nancy's eyebrows arched in mock surprise. "Oh? That was over twenty-four hours ago. You seem to be slowing down. I suppose you'll be including the near plane crash in your TV crime report tonight."

Allison's plastic smile faded, but only by a millimeter. "Come on, Nancy. I have my job and you have yours. Mine is to report the news. What's yours?"

Nancy ignored the obvious insult. "You lied to me, Allison. I thought we agreed that anything I told you about the Crown case was to remain strictly confidential."

Allison gave a careless shrug. Her smile remained intact. "There must have been some misunderstanding on your part, Nancy. At any rate, I'm convinced that the Crown case could develop into big news at any time. I'm giving it top priority. In fact, I've set up an appointment to interview Karen Crown. You met with her today, didn't you?"

Nancy tried not to show her surprise. "You don't drive a white sedan, do you?"

"What's that supposed to mean?" Allison asked in a puzzled voice.

"I'm just wondering if you aren't following me in the hopes of getting a story for your Channel Ten crime spot."

Allison was clearly indignant. "I'm very capable of finding my own stories without any help from you, Nancy Drew!" The TV reporter turned angrily on her heel and marched away.

Nancy was both annoyed and amused by her run-in with Allison Phillips.

At five o'clock Nancy picked Bess up at the photography studio. She was anxious to stop by the Morrises' house to check on Al Morris's condition, but Bess talked her into first grabbing a soda in the coffee shop next door to the studio.

Nancy sighed as she stirred the ice in her glass with a straw. "I hate to admit it, but I think I wasted the whole afternoon. I didn't really learn anything new."

"Don't worry, Nancy," Bess said brightly. "It's only a matter of time. Something will turn up soon. I know it will."

Nancy smiled. Her friend's words renewed Nancy's confidence in herself. Feeling more relaxed now, Nancy said, "Oh, I forgot to tell you, I saw Allison Phillips while I was at the newspaper office."

Bess made a sour face. "Do you have to mention *that* name while I'm eating?"

"I waited until you finished eating." Nancy laughed. Then she said, "Bess, before I take you home, would you mind driving over to Mrs. Morris's house with me?"

Nancy had already filled Bess in on her suspicions about the guard's drugging himself during the night of the robbery. When they arrived at the Morris home, Nancy pulled up next to the front curb. After one look at the Morrises' house and its surroundings, Bess remarked, "This isn't the best neighborhood in River Heights, is it?"

"No," Nancy replied, "it isn't."

"Why don't I wait in the car for you, Nancy?"

"Okay. I'll only be a few minutes," Nancy promised.

Mrs. Morris seemed pleased to see Nancy. She invited her in at once. "Nancy, it's nice of you to stop by. I only wish I had better news to report. Al is still in a coma."

Nancy reached out to give the older woman a hug. "I'm sorry to hear that, Mrs. Morris." Nancy hesitated before she asked, "You know that I'm investigating the Roget diamond robbery?"

Mrs. Morris nodded. "Yes, I understand that, my dear." She lowered her head sadly. "You believe Al had something to do with the robbery, don't you?"

"I'm sorry," Nancy replied gently, "but I think it's very possible."

"It must be true then," Mrs. Morris said. "Something's been bothering Al for months. He hasn't been himself since the night of the robbery."

"Mrs. Morris, do you have a sample of Al's handwriting?"

Mrs. Morris walked slowly to an old scarred desk in the far corner of the room. "Al was writing out bills just a few days ago." She sorted through a stack of papers on the desk. "Here." She held out a sheet of blue notepaper. "Al was writing to the telephone company. He thought they had overcharged us."

Nancy took the paper and inspected it closely. The paper and the handwriting were identical to the note that Mrs. Crown had received! She thanked Mrs. Morris and hurried out of the house. She was still on the front porch when she spotted the white sedan. With a roar the car tore off down the street.

Nancy raced to her car. She leaped into the driver's seat and reached for the keys in the ignition. They were gone. It was then that Nancy realized that Bess had disappeared!

12

Intensive Scare

The sedan turned the corner on two wheels and disappeared from sight. Realizing that Bess must have been forced into the car, Nancy frantically started to run back toward the Morris house. She had to notify the police at once!

Nancy was halfway across the front lawn when she heard someone calling her name. She stopped and looked across the street. It was Bess! Carrying an ice cream cone in either hand, she started to jog toward Nancy.

"Nancy, what is it? What's wrong? You look like you've seen a ghost."

"Bess!" Nancy was so glad to see her friend that she grabbed her by the shoulders and hugged her. "Bess, where have you been? I thought you had been kidnapped!"

Bess's eyes grew large. "Kidnapped! Why would you think that?"

"Didn't you see the white car? It must have been following us. When I came out of the Morris house it raced down the street and out of sight."

Bess handed Nancy an ice cream cone. "I didn't see anything, Nancy. A few minutes ago I heard the ice cream truck down at the far corner. I didn't want to leave your keys in the car, so I took them with me and went over to get us a couple of high-calorie goodies."

Nancy sighed as Bess handed her a cone with a double scoop of chocolate. "Bess, we just had sodas."

Bess polished off the top scoop of her cone. "I know. This is dessert."

Nancy grinned. "Bess, you're hopeless," she said, taking a large bite out of her own ice cream cone.

As they drove back to town Bess said, "Have you ever been able to make out any of the numbers on the white car's license plates?"

"Today is as close as I've come to that car. I realized for the first time that it doesn't have any plates. It must be a brand-new car. There was a sticker in the front windshield."

She added, "I did get some evidence from Mrs. Morris, though." Nancy pulled Al Morris's note from her pocket and handed it to Bess.

Bess inspected it carefully. "It looks like the note that was written to Mrs. Crown. Is this the same paper and the same handwriting?"

"I think so. The first thing I plan to do when I

get home is to compare the two notes, but I'm positive they're identical."

"I bet Al Morris is the jewel thief!" Bess declared excitedly.

Nancy shook her head. "No, Al Morris just let the jewel thief inside Roget's that night. But he knows who the thief is. The person we're after is whoever is driving that white car."

After Nancy dropped Bess off, she drove home. The first thing she did was to carefully study the two notes. Just as she had thought, the stationery and the scratchy blue handwriting were identical.

At six-thirty Nancy picked up her father at the airport. After they had collected his luggage and were settled in the car Nancy said, "Did you have a good trip, Dad?"

"Yes," Carson Drew replied. "My law partners are going to be very pleased with the way things worked out." He smiled at Nancy. "I hope your case is working out well, too. Has anything developed since I left?"

Nancy couldn't help but laugh at that question. She told her father about Larry Holtz's sabotaged plane, Al Morris's near confession, and her latest run-in with the white sedan.

Carson Drew smiled, but his eyes were filled with concern. "I see things have been as exciting here as always. I just hope you're being very careful, Nancy."

Nancy understood her father's concern. "Don't worry, Dad. I'm not taking any chances."

114

"Oh, by the way," Mr. Drew said, "I went to see Mrs. Crown's publishers. I have a copy of the manuscript she was working on just before she disappeared. It's in my briefcase."

The instant they arrived home Nancy started to read the manuscript. Since it was only partially completed, it took her only an hour to skim it. "I'm disappointed," Nancy admitted to her father. "It's about everything that has happened so far. A rich woman's daughter is jailed for a crime she didn't commit. The rich woman hires a detective and then suddenly vanishes from sight. That's it—nothing more."

Carson Drew nodded. "I was afraid you wouldn't find any real clues in the manuscript. I read it on the plane. I think Monica Crown is writing the book in the hope that it will draw out the real thief."

"You're right, Dad. Mrs. Crown let everyone know she was writing a book about the Roget diamond robbery. She's using the book as bait. Once it's published, she hopes it will lure the actual thief out into the open." Suddenly Nancy thought of something.

"Dad, could you do me a favor? Call Chief McGinnis. I think he should know about Al Morris's two notes."

"I'll be happy to," Mr. Drew replied, "but where are you going?"

Nancy was headed for the hall closet to get her trenchcoat. "Visiting hours aren't over at the hospital yet. I'd like to go over and see if Al Morris is any better."

"Now, would you do *me* a favor?" Mr. Drew asked his daughter.

Nancy smiled. "Sure, Dad. What is it?"

"Please take George and Bess along with you. The Roget thief will think twice before he tries to attack three people."

Nancy laughed. "You think there's safety in numbers even if one of them is Bess Marvin?"

Nancy put down the trenchcoat, went upstairs to her room, and dialed George's number. George picked up the phone on the second ring. "Would you mind doing something for me?" Nancy asked her friend. "I'm going to drive over to check on Al Morris at the hospital. If I can get you and Bess to drive along with me, I'd feel better. I don't think the Roget thief would try anything unless I'm alone."

Nancy could picture George's grin when she replied, "Nancy, I can understand why you might ask me to come along. I could at least hit someone over the head with my tennis racket, but Bess?"

Nancy laughed. "Bess would help me out if she really had to. Anyway, you have to admit she's got a good set of lungs."

"You're right." George giggled. "Bess has a scream that could alert the whole city. Why don't I give her a call. We'll come over and pick you up. If the weirdo in the white car is anywhere around, let's give him another car to tail."

116

"That's a good idea," Nancy agreed. "Thanks, George."

When the three girls entered the hospital lobby later, Nancy recognized Tom Owens stepping out of the elevator. "Tom, it's nice to see you again."

Tom Owens smiled and shook hands with Nancy. "Nancy, how have you been?" He nodded a friendly hello to George. Pulling the collar of his overcoat closer around him, Tom Owens said, "If you're here to see Al, forget it. I came to pay him a visit. He's a good friend—there's no nicer guy. I just hope he recovers.

"Anyway," he told Nancy, "the doctors aren't allowing him any visitors."

Bess stared at Tom Owens as he strode out of the lobby. "You two weren't kidding. He is very good-looking."

"But as we said before, he's much too old for you," George told her cousin. She pulled Bess's arm. "Stop staring. Nancy, we'll wait for you down here." Both George and Bess found a magazine and settled down in the lobby as Nancy took the elevator to the third floor. When she got out of the elevator she went straight to the third-floor desk. A cheerful nurse informed her that Al Morris's condition had improved somewhat during the past few hours. "But I'm afraid you won't be able to see Mr. Morris for a while. There's a doctor with him right now."

Nancy nodded. "Thank you. I'll wait."

Nancy found a chair in the hallway near the

117

room. When a doctor finally emerged from the room, Nancy hurried after him. "Excuse me, doctor. I'm a friend of Mr. Morris. Can you tell me how he's doing?"

The doctor was obviously in a rush. He continued down the corridor as he answered Nancy's question. "He's improved slightly. He's out of the coma, at least for the time being. He's heavily sedated, so he can't have any visitors at this time. I'm sorry."

Nancy was disappointed with this last bit of news. "I see," she replied. "Thank you, doctor." The doctor gave a wave and entered another patient's room. Nancy's words echoed in the lonely hallway.

She started back toward the elevator. She pressed the down button and waited. Suddenly she saw another doctor enter Al Morris's room. Only this doctor was wearing a surgical mask and gown. Why would a doctor need a surgical mask to enter the room? Nancy wondered. It seemed very suspicious. She hurried down the corridor, pushed the door to Al Morris's room open, and stepped inside.

The room was dark except for a faint glow coming from the night light above an empty bed. A screen separated the empty bed from Al Morris's bed. Without hesitating, Nancy rushed to Al Morris's side of the room. The man wearing the surgical mask and gown was bent over the sick man's sleeping form. There was a strange gasping sound. Nancy realized that the "doctor" was holding a pillow over Al Morris's face. He was trying to suffocate him!

"Stop that!" Nancy yelled. "You're going to kill him!"

The masked man, taken by surprise, dropped the pillow and started for Nancy. Before she was able to run or scream for help, a powerful hand clamped over her mouth. With his other arm the man grabbed Nancy around the throat and shoulder.

The attacker pushed her toward an open window. Nancy used every ounce of strength to fight him off, but it was useless. He was much larger and stronger than she was. Because he had gripped her tightly from behind, Nancy was unable to use any of her karate skills. Nancy's feet lifted off the floor as the attacker began to push her out the window. His grip around her mouth loosened as he shoved her farther outside. Nancy tumbled out of the window. She barely managed to grab the ledge with her hands as she fell.

With her body now dangling from the third-story window, Nancy started to scream for help. Clinging to the window ledge, she saw that far below a small crowd had started to gather. The attacker smashed the fingers of her left hand with his fist. Nancy cried out in pain. Her left hand fell to her side. Now the only thing between Nancy and certain death was the weakening grip of her right hand desperately clinging to the window ledge!

13

Tracking the Attacker

Just as the masked man was about to force Nancy to release her grip by crushing her fingers, a night nurse entered the hospital room. With the intruder distracted, Nancy painfully swung up her left arm and fumbled for a handhold.

"What's going on here?" the nurse demanded. When she saw Nancy's hands on the window ledge, she let out an ear-piercing scream.

The attacker turned and gave the nurse a violent shove as he fled from the room. The nurse landed on the hard linoleum and continued to scream. Within seconds the small room was crowded with members of the hospital staff. Several curious patients even left their sickbeds to see what was going on.

Strong hands grasped Nancy around both of her wrists. She was pulled to safety by the same doctor she had spoken to earlier in the corridor.

A hospital attendant helped the night nurse to her feet. After the nurse was led from the room, Nancy took several deep breaths to calm herself. Finally, she said to the doctor, "A man dressed as a doctor was trying to smother Al Morris! He had a pillow on his face when I came in here!"

The doctor immediately rushed to Al Morris's bedside and took charge of the whole situation. "I'll check the patient. In the meantime I'd like everyone else out of here. Liz," he said to the head nurse, "call the police at once. Then take this girl, and anyone else who saw anything, to the conference room."

"Just come with me, dear." The head nurse put a comforting arm around Nancy.

Nancy was still a little shaky, but she managed a smile. "I'm okay. Why don't you just tell me where the conference room is?"

"Go to the end of the hall and turn right," the nurse directed her.

Just before she reached the end of the hall, Nancy nearly collided with Frederick Reese, who was coming out of the men's room. "Mr. Reese!" Nancy exclaimed.

"If it isn't the girl detective my sister hired." Frederick Reese made no effort to be friendly. Nancy could see a definite resemblance between Mr. Reese and his son, Paul. Father and son were equally rude. "What are you up to now?" Mr. Reese asked in a demanding voice.

"I came here to visit Al Morris," Nancy replied.

Frederick Reese said angrily, "What you really mean is that you came here to question him. The poor man is half-dead. Can't you wait at least a few days before you start to harass him about the night of the robbery?"

Nancy's strength had returned. In a rare display of temper, she snapped back at Mr. Reese, "I did not come to harass him! For your information, Mr. Morris *asked* to talk to me."

Nancy continued in the direction of the conference room. Mr. Reese stepped in front of her, blocking her way. In a tired but much kinder voice he said, "I'm sorry, Ms. Drew, I really am."

Nancy's eyes widened in surprise at his sudden change of attitude.

"I'm here to visit Al, too," Mr. Reese said. "He's worked for me for over thirty years. His illness, along with my sister's disappearance and the whole business of the diamond robbery, has put me on edge."

Nancy said quietly, "That's all right, Mr. Reese. I understand." She watched Frederick Reese walk down the hall. It occurred to her that he was about the same height and size as the masked attacker. Maybe his apology was just a way to keep her from being suspicious.

When the hallway was clear, Nancy darted into the men's room. She quickly checked each stall and wastepaper basket. If Frederick Reese had been wearing the mask and gown, he hadn't stashed it in there.

Nancy was just replacing the contents of one of

the wastepaper baskets when a man entered. His mouth dropped open. "Hey, you lost or something, lady? This is the men's room."

Nancy flushed. "No . . . er . . . I mean . . . yes. I guess I didn't read the sign correctly. I thought I was in the women's restroom. Sorry." She rushed out the door.

There were already a number of people, including George and Bess, in the conference room by the time Nancy arrived. "What are you two doing here?" she asked.

"One of the nurses just told us what happened," George replied.

"We got worried waiting downstairs," Bess explained. "We came up to see if you were all right. Then the nurse told us about . . ." Bess looked upset. "Nancy, you could have been killed."

Nancy tried to reassure her two friends. "I'm okay, really. But it was pretty awful. I—" Nancy was interrupted by the all-too-familiar sight of Allison Phillips. The TV reporter had barged, uninvited, into the conference room. A few steps behind her a cameraman was adjusting a zoom lens for a close-up picture of Nancy.

Allison spoke in the same excited, overly dramatic voice she used on the news show. "I can't believe my good luck. Jason and I were just returning from an assignment. As we passed the hospital in the news van, I just happened to look up and see someone hanging from a third-story window! Unfortunately, we don't have pictures of you clinging to the window ledge, Nancy." Allison stopped long enough to frown at the cameraman. "Jason didn't have film in the camera. By the time he finally got the camera loaded and ready, it was too late. You were already back inside. Believe me, Jason," Allison said angrily, "our producer is going to hear about this!"

Nancy, Bess, and George looked at each other and shook their heads slowly.

Checking to see that Jason had the camera rolling, Allison turned on her microphone. "Now, Nancy, I'd like you to tell our viewers exactly what happened here tonight."

"Hold on there, Ms. Phillips," Police Chief McGinnis said as he entered the room. "I want Nancy to give *me* a full account of everything that happened here tonight. I'd appreciate it if you'd take that camera outside." The chief held the door open for the cameraman.

"Jason, wait in the corridor," Allison ordered. She gave the chief her most winning smile. "You don't mind if I stay, do you, Chief? I'll be as quiet as a mouse, I promise."

"All right," the chief agreed. "You can stay and take notes, but please don't interrupt."

Surprisingly, Allison obeyed the chief's order. Without a single word she found a seat and waited with pen and pad poised.

Chief McGinnis said, "Before we start, I want to know who else we have here."

"These are my friends, Bess Marvin and George Fayne," Nancy said.

A young woman added, "And I'm Sally Hagen, the night nurse. I went in to check on Mr. Morris when I saw some insane masked man trying to shove this poor girl out the window. I screamed. Before I knew what was happening, I was pushed to the floor. I fell with such force that I don't believe my back will ever be the same. It was just the most awful experience—"

"Thank you, nurse." The chief cut her off. "I'll get the rest of your statement before I leave." He looked around the room. "Were there any other witnesses?"

The doctor who had pulled Nancy to safety said, "I arrived after I heard Sally screaming."

"I'm the only person who saw the masked man try to smother Al Morris," Nancy said, "and I believe that Ms. Hagen is the only witness to the intruder's attempt on my life."

The police interrogation continued for forty-five minutes. During all this time, Allison Phillips's pen never stopped scribbling on her notepad. "Do you suppose she's writing a book?" George whispered to Bess.

"I don't know," Bess whispered back. "Even the chief hasn't taken half as many notes. I can hardly wait to see tonight's news."

When Chief McGinnis was satisfied that he had gathered all the information surrounding both attempted murders, he said to the doctor, "I'll put an officer outside Morris's room. I want him guarded twenty-four hours a day."

To Nancy he said, "I'm going to have all three

of you girls escorted home. When you get to your house, Nancy, lock everything up tight."

Nancy nodded. "Don't worry, Chief, I plan to do just that."

On their way down to the main floor, Allison and her cameraman managed to squeeze into the elevator with Nancy, Bess, George, and the police officer who had been assigned to see them safely home. "Nancy, you said you couldn't identify the attacker, but surely you must have some idea of who it could have been," Allison said.

"I have narrowed down my list of suspects," Nancy told her.

"Oh?" Allison said eagerly. "Who are they?"

"You know I can't tell you that," Nancy responded.

George said, "Maybe you'd like Nancy to hang outside the third-story window again now that you've got film in your camera."

Allison's eyes narrowed as she glared at George. Then she quickly flipped through her notes until she found George's name. "I think I should tell you two things, Ms. Fayne: sarcasm is a very unbecoming trait, and I am doing my job."

When the elevator door slid open Allison was the first one out. Under her breath, Bess said, "I get the feeling she doesn't like you, George."

"Oh, really?" George replied with a grin. "Whatever gave you that idea?"

Visiting hours were over, and the main lobby was nearly empty. Only a night janitor and an elderly woman occupied the room.

As she stepped out of the elevator, Nancy noticed the old woman rise off her chair and slowly walk toward her. She was bent over and appeared to be crippled. The old woman brushed against Nancy. As she did, she pressed a piece of paper into Nancy's hand. Nancy was able to get a glimpse of the woman's right hand. On her third finger she wore an emerald and gold ring in the shape of a dragon!

14

Two Mysteries Are Solved

Nancy's heart was pounding with excitement. It took every ounce of her self-control to remain silent during the long walk across the hospital parking lot, while they were within earshot of their escort. As soon as they were alone inside George's car, Nancy burst out, "Bess! George! I didn't want to say anything in front of the police officer, but look at this!" She held out her hand. "Guess what it is."

Bess and George both looked puzzled.

Unable to control her excitement any longer, Nancy cried, "It's a note from Mrs. Crown!"

"What!" Nancy's two friends chorused together.

"Did you notice the old woman in the lobby?"

"Are you telling us that *she* is Mrs. Crown?" George asked in disbelief.

Bess added, "But I thought Monica Crown was very attractive. In any picture I've ever seen of her she looks very sophisticated and stylish."

"She is!" Nancy laughed. "Don't you see— that was a disguise."

"Then how were you able to recognize her?" George asked.

"She wears a very unusual ring in the shape of a dragon."

"Come on, Nancy," Bess urged impatiently. "Hurry up and read the note. I can't wait to hear what it says."

Nancy was aware of the police car that had pulled up behind them. The officer was waiting to follow them home. She quickly snapped on the overhead light. She unfolded the paper and read the brief message aloud.

"Nancy, meet me tomorrow morning at ten o'clock. I'm staying at Willow Road Trailer Park, space 38. Also, please get word to Karen that I'm alive and well.

"Monica Crown"

"Nancy," Bess said, "would you mind if George and I went out to the trailer park with you? I'd love to meet Monica Crown!"

"Sure," Nancy replied as George pulled to a stop in front of the Drews' house. "I'll pick you both up in the morning." Nancy dashed up the walk and onto the front porch. Holding the door key in one hand she gave a wave to the police escort. Once she was safely inside, she heard the patrol car and George's car pull away from the curb.

"Nancy?" Mr. Drew called.

"Yes, Dad." Nancy started up the stairs to her room.

"How did everything go at the hospital tonight?"

Nancy laughed to herself. "It will take me awhile to tell you about that, Dad. I have a phone call to make first. I'll be back down to fill you in on everything in a few minutes."

It was a complicated procedure to convince the authorities at the prison to permit her to speak to Karen Crown so late at night. After identifying herself as the private detective who had visited Karen several days before, Nancy could hear someone on the other end of the line checking out this information on a computer.

Ten minutes later, Karen was on the phone. In an anxious voice she said, "Nancy?"

"Yes, Karen, I . . ."

"What is it? Is anything wrong? What's happened?"

Nancy laughed. It made her feel wonderful to finally have something good to report to Karen. "Karen, take a deep breath and relax. I have some good news for you. Your mother is alive!"

Nancy heard Karen's quick gasp. "But how—?" Nancy quickly told her about the note Mrs. Crown had given her. When she finished,

Karen said softly, "Thanks, Nancy. That's the best news I could have received."

The next morning, just before leaving for Willow Road Trailer Park, Nancy called Larry Holtz. When he answered the phone she said, "Larry, this is Nancy Drew. I remember that you told me you thought the Roget's diamonds were too 'hot' to fence."

"Yes," Larry replied. "I think the thief is holding on to them. It would be risky for him to try to get rid of them now. They're much too easy to recognize."

"But what if they've been cut?" Nancy asked.

Larry hesitated, "Well . . . in that case, they would be very difficult to identify. But you have to realize, Nancy, that the thief would risk getting caught if he took those diamonds to a stone-cutter."

Nancy felt a surge of excitement race through her. She was on the right track at last! "Thanks, Larry. You've been very helpful." Before she hung up, she told him about her call to Karen. Then she added, "And I think I'm going to have some more good news soon."

Nancy stopped by the Marvin and Fayne homes to pick up Bess and George. The three girls drove several miles outside of town to the small rundown trailer park that Mrs. Crown had mentioned in her note. They turned off the main highway and onto a narrow dirt road that led to the trailer park entrance.

"Okay," Nancy said. "We're looking for number thirty-eight."

"There it is," George pointed to an old, small mobile home that had seen better days.

Nancy parked her car next to an ancient beige station wagon. She led the way up the steps to a sliding glass door, then rapped lightly on the glass.

Mrs. Crown was no longer in disguise. She wore a green silk pantsuit. She slid the door open. As the girls entered she quickly glanced around outside to see if they had been followed. "Thank you for being so prompt," she said, giving Nancy a warm handshake.

"Mrs. Crown, I am really glad to see you," Nancy said with a smile. "I'd like you to meet my two closest friends, Bess Marvin and George Fayne."

The three girls sat down on a couch. Mrs. Crown took the only chair in the cramped living quarters.

"Nancy," Mrs. Crown began, "I'm sure you must think I've made your investigation doubly hard by pulling my disappearing act, but you see, my dear, I really had no other choice. Only hours after you agreed to take the case, an attempt was made on my life. I felt that I had to fake my own death at once."

"That's okay, Mrs. Crown," Nancy said. "It was all very confusing at first, but when I heard about the black velvet material that was found

132

near the accident, I was convinced you were in hiding somewhere nearby."

"Did you let Karen know that I'm all right?" Mrs. Crown asked anxiously.

"Yes, I did." Nancy added reassuringly, "I guess I don't need to tell you how happy she was when I told her I had received a message from you. Karen's a strong person, Mrs. Crown. She's going to come out of this just fine."

"Yes, I believe she will," Mrs. Crown agreed. "She's very fortunate to have such a fine young fiancé. I'm sure Larry has helped give her the extra strength and encouragement she's needed these past months."

Mrs. Crown's next words were difficult for her. "I don't know if you've reached the same conclusion as I have, but I'm afraid I have to face the fact that Frederick is the person we're after."

George leaned forward. "You suspect Mr. Reese, your brother?"

Mrs. Crown nodded sadly. "Yes. Frederick, I've discovered, is in desperate need of money. He borrowed quite a large sum last year. Only two weeks ago he asked for another loan."

"I have to admit that for quite a while Mr. Reese was my main suspect, too," Nancy said, "but now I'm sure he isn't the person we're looking for."

Mrs. Crown's alert eyes searched Nancy's face for some clue. "Who is it you suspect, Nancy?"

Nancy's eyes sparkled with the thrill of finally

solving the Crown case. "There's only one man who had the motive, the opportunity, and the necessary skill to pull off the Roget diamond robbery so cleverly."

A creak on the step outside suddenly caught everyone's attention. A man holding a revolver slid the door open and stepped inside. "It sounds as if you're describing me, Ms. Nancy Drew!"

15

A Tricky Escape

Nancy felt her pulse quicken, but she replied calmly, "Yes, Tom. You are the person I'm describing. Your motive was the fact that you were no longer able to continue at your job. You had the opportunity, as a trusted employee at Roget's, to know when the diamonds would arrive, and you had the rare skill of an expert stonecutter. You were able to cut the diamonds and dispose of them quickly without causing any suspicion."

Tom Owens's handsome features were now overshadowed by the furious look in his eyes. He took a step toward Nancy. It had become obvious that Tom Owens was a man filled with bitterness and hatred. "If it hadn't been for you, I would have gotten away with it. When I first met you and saw how young you were, I thought it was a laugh—a teenage detective! It didn't take me long to realize that you are very good at what you do, Nancy."

Nancy didn't reply. She knew the situation was desperate. Grimly, but with her mind and entire body alert, she watched Tom Owens come closer.

He motioned toward her with his gun. "Get up."

Bess instinctively reached out to cover Nancy's wrist with her hand. "Nancy . . ." Bess's voice was unsteady.

Nancy felt totally helpless, but she forced a brave smile. "It's okay, Bess."

There was a cruel note in Tom Owens's laugh. "I have to give you credit, though. You've got nerve. Every one of you has maybe twenty minutes to live, and your detective friend is telling you it's okay."

"How did you find me?" Nancy asked. "I kept checking my rearview mirror. No one followed me here."

Tom grinned. "I ran out of the room last night, but I didn't leave the hospital. There was so much going on, no one noticed an extra doctor in a mask and gown. Like you, I saw Monica in the waiting room. Even though she was disguised, I recognized her. I followed her here to the trailer park. I knew it would be only a matter of time before you showed up."

"Tom." Mrs. Crown started to get up.

Tom Owens pushed the older woman into her seat. "Sit down!" He waved the gun around dangerously. "The only person I want right now is you." The gun was pointed at Nancy. She rose and took slow cautious steps toward the man.

Mrs. Crown remained seated when she spoke again. "Tom, you've got to listen to me! I'm a wealthy woman. I can make it worth your while to let us go."

"Shut up, Monica!" Tom Owens seemed to be losing control. He gave Nancy a shove that sent her halfway across the room. "There's some rope on the porch. Get it!"

Nancy did as she was told. Tom pulled a knife from his pocket. He handed it to Nancy. "Cut the rope into four equal parts." Nancy again did as she was instructed. When the rope was cut, Tom pointed to George. "Her first—and make sure you tie her securely."

As Nancy tied George's hands the two girls exchanged a look that acknowledged their deep affection for one another. Nancy wanted to cry when she saw the look of sheer terror on Bess's face. When she finished tying her hands, Nancy gave Bess's arm a squeeze. Still filled with fear, Bess managed one brief, caring smile for her friend.

When Nancy had finished tying up Mrs. Crown, Tom Owens ordered her to turn around. He quickly bound Nancy's hands behind her back. He then took a box of wide tape from his coat pocket. He tore off four strips and covered the mouth of each of his prisoners. With a satisfied smile, he said, "That's to keep you ladies quiet. When the show begins I'm afraid you might want to scream."

Nancy wanted to scream now, more in outrage than in fear. She would not allow this madman to kill four innocent people.

Tom Owens used the last of the tape to wrap around his victims' ankles. He carelessly tossed the tape dispenser and knife on the floor. Then he pulled an explosive device from his pocket. Nancy immediately saw that it was similar to the one he had attached to her mailbox.

As if reading her mind, Tom said, "This is much larger and more destructive than the device I rigged to your mailbox. I'm going to place this under the curtains. You'll hear a small explosion in exactly three minutes. The curtains will catch fire first, then it's a matter of minutes before everything in here goes up in flames. But don't worry. If it's any consolation, you'll die of smoke inhalation before the flames reach you."

The instant Tom Owens was out the door, Nancy moved into action. She scooted as close to George as possible. With her eyes she managed to convey to George what she wanted her to do. George was able, with the tips of her fingers, to get hold of a tiny edge of the tape that covered Nancy's mouth. With her fingertips and Nancy's maneuvering, the tape was peeled off in seconds.

"We have about two minutes," Nancy said quickly. "I've tied each of you with a magician's knot. If I can get hold of the correct section of the

138

knot with my teeth, I should be able to pull the rope free. You first, George."

Nancy took the top section of the rope between her teeth. She pulled with all her strength. As if by magic, the rope loosened. George was free.

"George," Nancy said. "Get the knife and cut the tape around our ankles."

George quickly picked up the knife that Tom Owens had left behind. At the same instant the explosive device went off with a soft but ominous pop. The curtains went up in flames. George slashed the tape that was wrapped tightly around her own ankles. She raced to Mrs. Crown, who was the person closest to her, and quickly cut the tape that bound her. She repeated this procedure two more times.

Flames now engulfed the room. Coughing and gasping for breath, Nancy led the way down the narrow hallway to the back of the trailer. With her hands still tied, she was unable to open the rear door, but George gave it such a forceful push that it nearly flew off its hinges.

The four women ran to the nearest trailer. From there they called the fire department and Chief McGinnis at the police station.

Half an hour later, Nancy's blue sportscar pulled onto the gravel driveway of Tom Owens's house. Four police cars were already parked at the end of the lane. Uniformed officers with guns drawn had surrounded the house. Also parked at the end of the lane was a Channel 10 news van.

In the midst of all the confusion, Allison Phillips was scurrying about, trying her best to interview Chief McGinnis.

"Oh, no . . ." George groaned when she spotted the TV reporter.

"Now, George, let's not have any sarcasm from you. It is a very unbecoming trait," Bess told her cousin in a voice that mimicked Allison Phillips.

Both Nancy and George laughed at Bess's impersonation. Nancy said, "You've got to give Allison credit. She does have a nose for news!"

The girls and Mrs. Crown stayed near Nancy's car at a safe distance from the action. Nancy would have preferred to move in closer, but she felt she shouldn't interfere with what was now clearly police business.

Nancy couldn't help but smile when she heard the chief shout angrily, "Ms. Phillips, if you don't remove yourself and that cameraman from this area, I'll have you both arrested for obstructing justice!"

As she backed away from the scene, Allison spoke directly into the TV camera. "To my viewers, I just want to assure you that the Channel Ten news spot will continue to keep you informed and updated on what appears to be a major and fast-breaking story related to the Roget robbery and the recent disappearance of River Heights' most famous citizen, mystery writer Monica Crown." Just as Allison gave the signal to her ever-present coworker, Jason, to switch off the camera, she spotted Nancy. She hurried over to the young detective's side. "Well, Nancy, it's about time you showed up. It looks as if the police are about to capture the person you've been after." Allison's smile broadened as she added with obvious pleasure, "It's just too bad you weren't able to crack this case yourself. I suppose that whoever it is they've surrounded in there will be able to lead us to poor Monica Crown's body."

"The person they've surrounded in that house is Tom Owens," Nancy informed the TV reporter. "Mr. Owens just tried to kill four people. You'll want this information for your crime spot, Allison, so just make sure you get our names straight. Less than one hour ago, Tom Owens tried to kill me, my two friends, Bess Marvin and George Fayne, and"—Nancy paused and smiled at her client—"Monica Crown."

The fake smile that Allison constantly wore gave way to an expression of disbelief. For a single, wonderful moment, Allison Phillips was speechless. When she recovered from her shock, the smile was back in place. "Well . . . I . . . Mrs. Crown, I'm so happy to see you. I'm one of your greatest fans. Everyone has been very concerned since the night of your disappearance." Allison's smile faded only slightly as she barked over her shoulder, "Jason! Get the camera ready. I want to interview Mrs. Crown." To Monica Crown she said sweetly, "Mrs. Crown, would you be kind enough to—"

"Perhaps later, Ms. Phillips," Mrs. Crown cut

the reporter off abruptly. "Right now I want to see what is going on at the house."

Chief McGinnis called through a bullhorn, "This is your last chance, Owens. Save us all a lot of trouble and come out with your hands up."

Finally realizing that his situation was hopeless, Tom Owens opened the front door. He stepped out on the porch with his hands above his head. As he walked toward the chief, he caught sight of Nancy, Bess, George, and Mrs. Crown. He halted and stared at them in stunned silence.

Nancy and the others moved closer as the chief pulled Owens's hands behind his back and snapped on a pair of handcuffs. Tom looked at the four women. "Do you mind telling me how you got away?" He spoke to Nancy.

Nancy replied with just a trace of a smile. "You might say our escape was a sort of magic trick, Mr. Owens."

As he started to walk past her, Nancy said, "Now would you answer a question for me? Where do you keep your white sedan?"

Tom Owens refused to meet Nancy's eyes with his own. With his head cast downward, he muttered, "You'll find it out back in the barn."

The chief's car took off, its sirens blaring. Mrs. Crown shook her head slowly and said, "I always liked Tom. I find it hard to believe that he'd let Karen go to prison for his crime—or that he'd try to kill us."

"I know," Nancy said sadly. "He's so good-looking and charming. I liked him when I first met him, too. I guess what they say is true."

"What's that, Nancy?" George asked.

"You can't judge a book by its cover," Nancy replied.

Mrs. Crown managed a rueful smile. "Speaking of books, I can thank Tom for one thing. He's given me a lot of material for my next one!"

16

Happy Ending

To celebrate Karen's release from prison and the conclusion to the Roget diamond mystery, Mrs. Crown threw a big party. Carson Drew drove his car through the gated entrance that led to the Crown mansion. Nancy was seated between her father and Ned in the front seat. Bess and George sat in the backseat.

The housekeeper, Mrs. Adams, was on hand to greet them at the door and to lead them into the large formal dining room, where most of the guests had already gathered.

When Mrs. Crown saw Carson and Nancy Drew and their friends, she excused herself from the small group with whom she had been chatting. She welcomed Carson Drew with a warm handshake, and greeted Bess and George. To Nancy she extended both hands. "My dear, I'm so delighted to see you." Now that her life had returned to normal, Mrs. Crown seemed much younger and radiantly happy.

"Mrs. Crown," Nancy said, bringing Ned forward. "I'd like you to meet my boyfriend, Ned Nickerson."

Mrs. Crown smiled at Ned. "I'm very happy to meet you." She put an arm around Nancy. "And I hope you realize what a prize you have here."

Ned smiled back at Mrs. Crown. "I've always known Nancy was special."

So many compliments were making Nancy uncomfortable. To change the subject, she said, "Karen looks terrific."

It was true. A healthy color had returned to Karen's cheeks, and she seemed to glow with happiness. With her arm linked in Larry's, she walked toward Nancy. Karen said, "I'm really glad you could come tonight, Nancy. I owe you so much. I want you to know how grateful I am for everything you've done."

"It was really Al Morris who brought the whole case to a head," Nancy replied. "If he hadn't wanted to clear his conscience, Tom Owens might have gotten away with the diamond theft."

"I hear that Al is getting better every day," Karen said. "My uncle Frederick is planning to recommend leniency when the Roget case goes to trial."

Nancy saw Frederick and Paul Reese across the room. After everything that had happened she was surprised to see them at Mrs. Crown's party.

Mrs. Crown guessed what Nancy was thinking. "Both my brother and nephew have disappointed me during this whole ordeal, but they are family, and I still care about them both."

"I understand," Nancy said gently.

"My plane has been repaired," Larry Holtz told Nancy and Ned. "I don't suppose you two would like to go up again soon?"

Nancy and Ned exchanged a look before they both grinned and shook their heads. "You supposed right, Larry." Nancy laughed.

Nancy introduced Karen and Larry to her father and her friends. "Mr. Drew," Karen said, "was it you who taught Nancy how to tie a magician's knot? Mother tells me that was what saved her life."

"Actually," Mr. Drew replied, "that was a trick a family friend who was an amateur magician taught Nancy when she was about nine or ten years old."

"It's come in handy more than once since then," Nancy said.

"Well, it's a good thing you knew it," George put in. "If you hadn't, I hate to think what might have happened to us."

"I really wish we could talk about something more pleasant than that horrible morning!" Bess looked grim.

Nancy smiled. "You're right, Bess. But first, I just want to say that I spoke to Chief McGinnis today. He told me that Tom Owens admitted cutting the stolen Roget's diamonds into several smaller stones. Owens named the buyers, and they were jailed today."

"And I have some good news I'd like to share with all of you," Mrs. Crown announced. "During the last few days I've been busy writing the plot outline for a new mystery novel. The book will deal with a jewel theft, a falsely accused victim, and"—Mrs. Crown paused and smiled fondly at Nancy—"a brilliant teenage detective."

Nancy laughed. "Sounds like a good book to me. Can I buy the first copy?"

OVER THREE MILLION PAPERBACKS SOLD IN FIVE YEARS!
WHICH OF THESE MYSTERY BOOKS ARE YOU
MISSING FROM YOUR COLLECTION?

THE HARDY BOYS® SERIES
By Franklin W. Dixon

	ORDER NO.	PRICE	QUANTITY
NIGHT OF THE WEREWOLF—#59	62480	$3.50	
MYSTERY OF THE SAMURAI SWORD—#60	95497	$3.50	
THE PENTAGON SPY—#61	95570	$3.50	
THE APEMAN'S SECRET—#62	62479	$3.50	
THE MUMMY CASE—#63	41111	$3.50	
MYSTERY OF SMUGGLERS COVE—#64	41112	$3.50	
THE STONE IDOL—#65	62626	$3.50	
THE VANISHING THIEVES—#66	63890	$3.50	
THE OUTLAW'S SILVER—#67	64285	$3.50	
DEADLY CHASE—#68	62477	$3.50	
THE FOUR-HEADED DRAGON—#69	42341	$3.50	
THE INFINITY CLUE—#70	62475	$3.50	
TRACK OF THE ZOMBIE—#71	62623	$3.50	
THE VOODOO PLOT—#72	64287	$3.50	
THE BILLION DOLLAR RANSOM—#73	42355	$3.50	
TIC-TAC-TERROR—#74	42357	$3.50	
TRAPPED AT SEA—#75	64290	$3.50	
GAME PLAN FOR DISASTER—#76	64288	$3.50	
THE CRIMSON FLAME—#77	64286	$3.50	
CAVE-IN—#78	62621	$3.50	
SKY SABOTAGE—#79	62625	$3.50	
THE ROARING RIVER MYSTERY—#80	63823	$3.50	
THE DEMON'S DEN—#81	62622	$3.50	
THE BLACKWING PUZZLE—#82	62624	$3.50	
THE SWAMP MONSTER—#83	55048	$3.50	
REVENGE OF THE DESERT PHANTOM—#84	49729	$3.50	
SKYFIRE PUZZLE—#85	49731	$3.50	
THE MYSTERY OF THE SILVER STAR—#86	64374	$3.50	
THE HARDY BOYS® GHOST STORIES	50808	$3.50	
NANCY DREW® AND THE HARDY BOYS® CAMP FIRE STORIES	50198	$3.50	
NANCY DREW® AND THE HARDY BOYS® SUPER SLEUTHS	43375	$3.50	
NANCY DREW® AND THE HARDY BOYS® SUPER SLEUTHS #2	50194	$3.50	

NANCY DREW®and THE HARDY BOYS®are trademarks of Simon & Schuster,
registered in the United States Patent and Trademark Office.

YOU WON'T HAVE A CLUE WHAT YOU'RE MISSING...UNTIL
YOU ORDER. NO RISK OFFER—RETURN ENTIRE PAGE TODAY

Simon & Schuster, Mail Order Dept. HB5
200 Old Tappan Road, Old Tappan, NJ 07675
Please send me copies of the books checked. (If not completely satisfied, return for full refund in 14 days.)

☐ Enclosed full amount per copy with this coupon
(Send check or money order only.)
Please be sure to include proper postage and handling:
95¢—first copy
50¢—each additonal copy ordered.

☐ If order is for $10.00 or more,
you may charge to one of the
following accounts:
☐ Mastercard ☐ Visa

Name _____ Credit Card No. _____

Address _____

City _____ Card Expiration Date _____

State _____ Zip _____ Signature _____

Books listed are also available at your local bookstore. Prices are subject to change without notice.

HBD-02

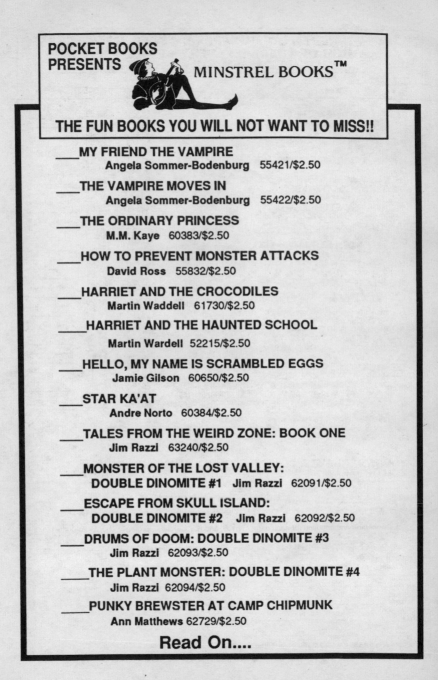

____THE DASTARDLY MURDER OF DIRTY PETE
    Eth Clifford 55835/$2.50

____ME, MY GOAT, AND MY SISTER'S WEDDING
    Stella Pevsner 62422/$2.50

____JUDGE BENJAMIN: THE SUPERDOG RESCUE
    Judith Whitelock McInerney 54202/$2.50

____DANGER ON PANTHER PEAK
    Bill Marshall 61282/$2.50

____THIRD PRIZE SURPRISE: BAD NEWS BUNNY #1
    Susan Saunders 62713/$2.50

____BACK TO NATURE: BAD NEWS BUNNY #2
    Susan Saunders 62714/$2.50

____STOP THE PRESSES!: BAD NEWS BUNNY #3
    Susan Saunders 62715/$2.50

____WHO'S GOT A SECRET?: BAD NEWS BUNNY #4
    Susan Saunders 62716/$2.50

____CAUGHT IN THE ACT: BAD NEWS BUNNY #5
    Susan Saunders 62717/$2.50

____ME AND THE TERRIBLE TWO
    Ellen Conford 63666/$2.50

____THE CASE OF THE HORRIBLE SWAMP MONSTER
    Drew Stevenson 62693/$2.50

____WHO NEEDS A BRATTY BROTHER?
    Linda Gondosh 62777/$2.50

____FERRET IN THE BEDROOM, LIZARDS IN THE FRIDGE
    Bill Wallace 63264/$2.50

Simon & Schuster Mail Order Department MMM
200 Old Tappan Rd., Old Tappan, N.J. 07675

Please send me the books I have checked above. I am enclosing $_____ (please add 75¢ to
cover postage and handling for each order. N.Y.S. and N.Y.C. residents please add appro-priate
sales tax). Send check or money order--no cash or C.O.D.'s please. Allow up to six weeks for
delivery. For purchases over $10.00 you may use VISA: card number, expiration date and
customer signature must be included.

Name _____

Address _____

City _____ State/Zip _____

VISA Card No. _____ Exp. Date _____

Signature _____ 702